WASHINGTON IRVING

SELECTED WRITINGS

WASHINGTON IRVING

SELECTED WRITINGS

a *Broadview Anthology of American Literature* edition

General Editors, *The Broadview Anthology of American Literature*

Derrick R. Spires, Cornell University
Rachel Greenwald Smith, Saint Louis University
Christina Roberts, Seattle University
Joseph Rezek, Boston University
Justine S. Murison, University of Illinois, Urbana-Champaign
Laura L. Mielke, University of Kansas
Christopher Looby, University of California, Los Angeles
Rodrigo Lazo, University of California, Irvine
Alisha Knight, Washington College
Hsuan L. Hsu, University of California, Davis
Michael Everton, Simon Fraser University
Christine Bold, University of Guelph

broadview press

BROADVIEW PRESS – www.broadviewpress.com
Peterborough, Ontario, Canada

Founded in 1985, Broadview Press remains a wholly independent publishing house. Broadview's focus is on academic publishing: our titles are accessible to university and college students as well as scholars and general readers. With over 800 titles in print, Broadview has become a leading international publisher in the humanities, with world-wide distribution. Broadview is committed to environmentally responsible publishing and fair business practices.

Library and Archives Canada Cataloguing in Publication

Title: Washington Irving : selected writings / general editors, The Broadview anthology of American literature: Derrick R. Spires (Cornell University), Rachel Greenwald Smith (Saint Louis University), Christina Roberts (Seattle University), Joseph Rezek (Boston University), Justine S. Murison (University of Illinois, Urbana-Champaign), Laura L. Mielke (University of Kansas), Christopher Looby (University of California, Los Angeles), Rodrigo Lazo (University of California, Irvine), Alisha Knight (Washington College), Hsuan L. Hsu (University of California, Davis), Michael Everton (Simon Fraser University), Christine Bold (University of Guelph).
Other titles: Works. Selections (2023)
Names: Irving, Washington, 1783-1859, author. | Container of (work): Irving, Washington, 1783-1859. History of New York. Selections. | Container of (work): Irving, Washington, 1783-1859. Sketch-book of Geoffrey Crayon, gent. Selections. | Spires, Derrick Ramon, editor.
Description: Series statement: A Broadview anthology of American literature edition | Includes bibliographical references.
Identifiers: Canadiana (print) 20230179304 | Canadiana (ebook) 20230179320 | ISBN 9781554816378 (softcover) | ISBN 9781770489066 (PDF) | ISBN 9781460408384 (EPUB)
Classification: LCC PS2053 .S65 2023 | DDC 813/.2—dc23

Broadview Press handles its own distribution in North America:
PO Box 1243, Peterborough, Ontario K9J 7H5, Canada
555 Riverwalk Parkway, Tonawanda, NY 14150, USA
Tel: (705) 743-8990; Fax: (705) 743-8353
email: customerservice@broadviewpress.com

For all territories outside of North America, distribution is handled by Eurospan Group.

Broadview Press acknowledges the financial support of the Government of Canada for our publishing activities.

Canada

Developmental Editor: Don LePan
Cover Designer: Lisa Brawn
Typesetter: Alexandria Stuart

PRINTED IN CANADA

Contents

Introduction

Washington Irving
1783 – 1859

Washington Irving was the United States' first literary celebrity, and among the first American writers to be widely read and respected—including in Britain, where critics had long scoffed at literature in America. Over the course of his highly varied career, Irving earned fame for his urbane satire and ambitious, pseudohistorical parody; for his small-scale literary portraits of rural New York; and for works of nonfiction that capitalized on the emerging cultural importance of the American "frontier." As an important advocate for writers' financial rights, and one of the first Americans to attain financial success through his writings alone, Irving played a vital role in giving shape to an American literary market—and stature to a national literature that was struggling for recognition.

Born to English and Scottish parents in Manhattan in 1783, Irving was raised primarily in the growing metropolis, but also experienced the landscapes and cultural heritage of rural Dutch New York, whose influence would be seen in some of his earliest writings. Though he was initially pushed toward a career in the law, Irving had by his early twenties established a local reputation as a satirist and occasional theater critic; he wrote a popular series of letters under the pen name of Jonathan Oldstyle for New York's *Morning Chronicle* in 1802, and from 1807 to 1808 collaborated with his brother William and friend James Kirke Paulding on the periodical *Salmagundi*, which was among the first publications to refer to New York City by the nickname "Gotham."

By 1809, Irving was piecing together his first major book, a unified work that quickly evolved from an extension of the satirical *Salmagundi* project into a work of much broader literary and cultural scope. Published late that year, *A History of New York, from the Beginning of the World to the End of the Dutch Dynasty* was a lively parody of American historical publications. Written in the persona of the elderly and rather unreliable Dutch historian Diedrich Knickerbocker, the book's account of New York's colonial history was composed of both farce and fact; though parodic in tone, the text was nevertheless based on serious archival research on Irving's part, and worked to feed the growing post-revolutionary hunger of Euro-Americans for an account of their national heritage. In this sense, Irving's *History* responded to the appeals of writers like Charles Brockden Brown, who had in the *American Review* of 1802 called for an American historian who could "vie with those who have so recently shone in Great-Britain." The *History* became the most lucrative single literary work yet published in the United States. Abroad, its humor won the admiration (and won Irving the friendship) of Scottish Romantic poet Sir Walter Scott, who claimed the volume had given him an "uncommon degree of entertainment," and who favorably compared Irving's writing to that of the famous satirists Jonathan Swift and Laurence Sterne. The immensely popular Scott would prove an important influence on Irving's later fiction.

Irving's next publication, written while he was living abroad in England, constituted a considerable change in his literary vision. The stories and sketches that made up *The Sketch Book of Geoffrey Crayon, Gent.* (1819–20) were written under yet another pseudonym. Lightly comic in tone, they also exhibited Irving's increasingly romantic sensibility and interest in European myth. Much of the text was inspired by Irving's recent readings of German folktales, to which he had been introduced by Scott; "Rip Van Winkle," for example, is an Americanized adaptation of the German tale "Peter Klaus."

The Sketch Book was published in the United States between 1819 and 1820 to extraordinary and lasting acclaim; years later, American poet Henry Wadsworth Longfellow would call the collection his "first book," "the one book among all others" that first captivated him as a child. *The Sketch Book* was soon re-published in Britain by the prestigious publisher John Murray. In an age of rampant and unchecked book piracy—especially when it came to international publication—Irving established a copyright in England and subsequently became one of the first American authors to make a profit from books printed abroad. The English volumes of *The Sketch Book* contained a number of both major and minor revisions, some likely designed to capitalize on the new literary market; particularly noteworthy were two added sketches depicting and commenting on Native American culture and life. In England, *The Sketch Book* was admired by writers such as Lord Byron and Charles Dickens; Irving's numerous tales of English Christmas traditions contributed to a tradition that would later influence Dickens's famous Christmas tales. Overall, indeed, *The Sketch Book*'s focus was almost overwhelmingly English—yet its most popularly enduring stories, "Rip Van Winkle" and "The Legend of Sleepy Hollow," have acquired near-mythic status as quintessentially American fables.

Irving's next two books, *Bracebridge Hall* (1822) and *Tales of a Traveller* (1824), were also written under the Geoffrey Crayon pseudonym and inspired by Irving's European travels. He then wrote *The Life and Voyages of Christopher Columbus* (1828) while on a political assignment in Madrid. Though a rather fanciful account of the explorer's life, the work long remained a standard educational text in American schools; as such, it contributed to an enduring historical misconception: the notion that Europeans had believed the earth to be flat until Columbus's voyage had proved them wrong.

After seventeen years abroad Irving finally returned to the United States and was recognized there as a celebrity. He embarked on a tour of the western regions of the country, which provided the raw material for three lucrative volumes of travel writing. These books— *A Tour on the Prairies* (1833), *Astoria: Or, Enterprise Beyond the Rocky Mountains* (1836), and *The Adventures of Captain Bonneville* (1837)— represent another significant shift in Irving's literary vision and cultural focus. Irving encourages his readers to take excursions into the west such as he had done. He wrote, in *A Tour*: "We send our youth abroad to grow luxurious and effeminate in Europe; it appears to me that a previous tour on the prairies would be more likely to produce that manliness, simplicity, and self-dependence most in unison with our political institutions." These books both contributed to and were shaped by the growing culture of western expansion—exemplified in fiction by the works of James Fenimore Cooper—with *A Tour* influentially describing the frontier as a place "between civilized and savage life." Though Irving shows some sympathy for the struggles of Indigenous Americans, he nevertheless portrays western expansion—reliant on the genocidal Indian Removal Act—in broadly romantic terms.

The travel volumes proved lucrative, and allowed Irving to purchase property in the region that has since 1996 been named Sleepy Hollow in his honor. He spent the last two decades of his life writing several biographical works, including a life of Irish writer Oliver Goldsmith (whose *Citizen of the World* [1760–61] Irving had admired as a child) and the substantial *Life of George Washington* (1855–59). Irving died a few months after the release of the latter work's final volume, and was buried in the cemetery at Sleepy Hollow. Upon Irving's death, the English novelist William Makepeace Thackeray described him as "the first ambassador whom the New World of Letters sent to the Old." In that so-called New World, Irving's work had bolstered and brought life to American literature as a whole, and the American short story in particular. Though American authors would continue throughout much of the nineteenth century to struggle against a literary market that privileged British writing, Irving helped open the door to the idea that American writers could be worth reading. His depictions of the American landscape, from the Hudson River and the Catskill Mountains to Oregon, helped define a whole set of romantic associations with those regions in America's popular imagination.

Note on the Text

Unless otherwise noted, the texts of the writings presented here have been prepared based on their first American editions: the 1809 edition of *A History of New York* and the 1819–20 editions of *The Sketch Book of Geoffrey Crayon, Gent.* Spelling and punctuation have been modernized in accordance with the practices of *The Broadview Anthology of American Literature.*

ℭℜ

from A HISTORY OF NEW YORK,
FROM THE BEGINNING OF THE
WORLD TO THE END OF THE
DUTCH DYNASTY, BY
DIEDRICH KNICKERBOCKER

The writer of a history may, in some respects, be likened unto an adventurous knight, who having undertaken a perilous enterprise, by way of establishing his fame, feels bound in honour and chivalry to turn back for no difficulty nor hardship, and never to shrink or quail whatever enemy he may encounter. Under this impression, I resolutely draw my pen and fall to, with might and main, at those doughty questions and subtle paradoxes, which, like fiery dragons and bloody giants, beset the entrance to my history, and would fain repulse me from the very threshold. And at this moment a gigantic question has started up, which I must take by the beard and utterly subdue before I can advance another step in my historic undertaking—but I trust this will be the last adversary I shall have to contend with, and that in the next book I shall be enabled to conduct my readers in triumph into the body of my work.

The question which has thus suddenly arisen is, what right had the first discoverers of America to land and take possession of a country, without asking the consent of its inhabitants, or yielding them an adequate compensation for their territory?

My readers shall now see with astonishment how easily I will vanquish this gigantic doubt, which has so long been the terror of adventurous writers, which has withstood so many fierce assaults, and has given such great distress of mind to multitudes of kind-hearted folks. For, until this mighty question is totally put to rest, the worthy people of America can by no means enjoy the soil they inhabit with clear right and title, and quiet, unsullied consciences.

The first source of right, by which property is acquired in a country, is discovery. For as all mankind have an equal right to anything which has never before been appropriated, so any nation that discovers an uninhabited country, and takes possession thereof, is considered as enjoying full property, and absolute, unquestionable empire therein.

This proposition being admitted, it follows clearly that the Europeans who first visited America were the real discoverers of the same, nothing being necessary to the establishment of this fact, but simply to prove that it was totally uninhabited by man. This would at first appear to be a point of some difficulty, for it is well known that this quarter of the world abounded with certain animals that walked erect on two feet, had something of the human countenance, uttered certain unintelligible sounds, very much like language; in short, had a marvellous resemblance to human beings. But the host of zealous and enlightened fathers, who accompanied the discoverers, for the purpose of promoting the kingdom of heaven, by establishing fat monasteries and bishoprics on Earth, soon cleared up this point, greatly to the satisfaction of his holiness the Pope, and of all Christian voyagers and discoverers.

They plainly proved—and as there were no Indian writers arose on the other side, the fact was considered as fully admitted and established—that the two-legged race of animals before mentioned, were mere cannibals, detestable monsters, and many of them giants—which last description of vagrants have, since the time of Gog, Magog, and Goliath,[1] been considered as outlaws, and have received no quarter in either history, chivalry or song; indeed, even the philosophic Bacon, declared the Americans to be people proscribed by the laws of nature, inasmuch as they had a barbarous custom of sacrificing men, and feeding upon man's flesh.

Nor are these all the proofs of their utter barbarism: among many other writers of discernment, the celebrated Ulloa[2] tells us, "their imbecility is so visible, that one can hardly form an idea of them different from what one has of the brutes. Nothing disturbs the tranquillity of their souls, equally insensible to disasters, and to prosperity. Though half naked, they are as contented as a monarch in his most splendid array. Fear makes no impression on them, and respect as little." All this is furthermore supported by the authority of M. Bouguer.[3] "It is not easy," says he, "to describe the degree of their indifference for wealth and all its advantages. One does not well know what motives to propose to them when one would persuade them to any service. It is vain to offer them money, they answer that they are not hungry." And Vanegas[4] confirms the whole, assuring us that "ambition, they have none, and are more desirous of being thought strong, than valiant. The objects of

---

1   *Gog, Magog and Goliath*   Monstrous beings from the Old Testament.
2   *Ulloa*   Spanish explorer of central America, Francisco de Ulloa (d. 1540).
3   *Bouguer*   Pierre Bouguer (1698–1758), French mathematician and astronomer who traveled to Peru.
4   *Vanegas*   Possibly Mexican Jesuit historian and ethnographical writer Miguel Venegas (1680–1764).

ambition with us, honour, fame, reputation, riches, posts and distinctions are unknown among them. So that this powerful spring of action, the cause of so much *seeming* good and *real* evil in the world has no power over them. In a word, these unhappy mortals may be compared to children, in whom the development of reason is not completed."

Now all these peculiarities—although in the unenlightened states of Greece, they would have entitled their possessors to immortal honour, as having reduced to practice those rigid and abstemious maxims, the mere talking about which, acquired certain old Greeks the reputation of sages and philosophers[1]—yet were they clearly proved in the present instance, to betoken a most abject and brutified nature, totally beneath the human character. But the benevolent fathers, who had undertaken to turn these unhappy savages into dumb beasts, by dint of argument, advanced still stronger proofs; for as certain divines of the sixteenth century and, among the rest, Lullus,[2] affirm—the Americans go naked, and have no beards! "They have nothing," says Lullus, "of the reasonable animal, except the mask." And even that mask was allowed to avail them but little, for it was soon found that they were of a hideous copper complexion—and being of a copper complexion, it was all the same as if they were negroes—and negroes are black, "and black," said the pious fathers, devoutly crossing themselves, "is the colour of the Devil!" Therefore, so far from being able to own property, they had no right even to personal freedom, for liberty is too radiant a deity to inhabit such gloomy temples. All which circumstances plainly convinced the righteous followers of Cortes and Pizarro,[3] that these miscreants had no title to the soil that they infested—that they were a perverse, illiterate, dumb, beardless, bare-bottomed *black-seed*—mere wild beasts of the forests, and like them should either be subdued or exterminated.

From the foregoing arguments therefore, and a host of others equally conclusive, which I forbear to enumerate, it was clearly evident, that this fair quarter of the globe, when first visited by

---

1   *having reduced ... philosophers* I.e., living the ascetic, unmaterialistic lifestyle that was praised by Greek philosophers but not fully practiced by them.

2   *Lullus* It is unclear to whom Irving is referring here.

3   *Cortes and Pizarro* Spanish conquistadors Hernán Cortés (1485–1547) and Francisco Pizarro (1471–1541), whose expeditions led to the destruction, respectively, of the Aztec and Incan Empires.

Europeans, was a howling wilderness, inhabited by nothing but wild beasts; and that the transatlantic visitors acquired an incontrovertible property therein, by the *right of Discovery*.

This right being fully established, we now come to the next, which is the right acquired by *cultivation*. "The cultivation of the soil," we are told, "is an obligation imposed by nature on mankind. The whole world is appointed for the nourishment of its inhabitants; but it would be incapable of doing it, was it uncultivated. Every nation is then obliged by the law of nature to cultivate the ground that has fallen to its share. Those people like the ancient Germans and modern Tartars, who having fertile countries, disdain to cultivate the earth, and choose to live by rapine,[1] are wanting to themselves, and *deserve to be exterminated as savage and pernicious beasts*."[2]

Now it is notorious, that the savages knew nothing of agriculture, when first discovered by the Europeans, but lived a most vagabond, disorderly, unrighteous life—rambling from place to place, and prodigally rioting upon the spontaneous luxuries of nature, without tasking her generosity to yield them anything more; whereas it has been most unquestionably shown, that heaven intended the earth should be ploughed and sown, and manured, and laid out into cities and towns and farms, and country seats, and pleasure grounds, and public gardens, all which the Indians knew nothing about—therefore they did not improve the talents providence had bestowed on them—therefore they were careless stewards—therefore they had no right to the soil—therefore they deserved to be exterminated.

It is true the savages might plead that they drew all the benefits from the land which their simple wants required—they found plenty of game to hunt, which together with the roots and uncultivated fruits of the earth, furnished a sufficient variety for their frugal table—and that as heaven merely designed the earth to form the abode, and satisfy the wants of man, so long as those purposes were answered, the will of heaven was accomplished. But this only proves how undeserving they were of the blessings around them—they were so much the more savages, for not having more wants; for knowledge is in some degree an increase of desires, and it is this superiority both

---

1 *Tartars* People from the central Asian area formerly known as Tartary; *rapine* Robbery, pillaging.

2 *The cultivation ... pernicious beasts* From Emer de Vattel's *The Law of Nations* (1758).

in the number and magnitude of his desires, that distinguishes the man from the beast. Therefore the Indians, in not having more wants, were very unreasonable animals; and it was but just that they should make way for the Europeans, who had a thousand wants to their one, and therefore would turn the earth to more account, and by cultivating it, more truly fulfil the will of heaven. Besides—Grotius and Lauterbach, and Puffendorf and Titius[1] and a host of wise men besides, who have considered the matter properly, have determined, that the property of a country cannot be acquired by hunting, cutting wood, or drawing water in it—nothing but precise demarcation of limits, and the intention of cultivation, can establish the possession. Now as the savages (probably from never having read the authors above quoted) had never complied with any of these necessary forms, it plainly follows that they had no right to the soil, but that it was completely at the disposal of the first comers, who had more knowledge and more wants than themselves—who would portion out the soil, with churlish boundaries; who would torture nature to pamper a thousand fantastic humours and capricious appetites; and who of course were far more rational animals than themselves. In entering upon a newly discovered, uncultivated country therefore, the newcomers were but taking possession of what, according to the aforesaid doctrine, was their own property—therefore in opposing them, the savages were invading their just rights, infringing the immutable laws of nature and counteracting the will of heaven—therefore they were guilty of impiety, burglary and trespass on the case—therefore they were hardened offenders against God and man—therefore they ought to be exterminated.

But a more irresistible right than either that I have mentioned, and one which will be the most readily admitted by my reader, provided he is blessed with bowels of charity and philanthropy, is the right acquired by civilization. All the world knows the lamentable state in which these poor savages were found. Not only deficient in the comforts of life, but what is still worse, most piteously and unfortunately blind to the miseries of their situation. But no sooner did the

---

1   *Grotius … Titius*   Irving lists several writers who (together with the even-more-influential John Locke) were leading figures in setting forth theories of property that provided the English—and other Europeans—with philosophical justifications for the colonization of lands formerly inhabited by Indigenous peoples.

benevolent inhabitants of Europe behold their sad condition than they immediately went to work to ameliorate and improve it. They introduced among them the comforts of life, consisting of rum, gin and brandy—and it is astonishing to read how soon the poor savages learnt to estimate these blessings—they likewise made known to them a thousand remedies, by which the most inveterate diseases are alleviated and healed, and that they might comprehend the benefits and enjoy the comforts of these medicines, they previously introduced among them the diseases, which they were calculated to cure. By these and a variety of other methods was the condition of these poor savages, wonderfully improved; they acquired a thousand wants, of which they had before been ignorant, and as he has most sources of happiness, who has most wants to be gratified, they were doubtlessly rendered a much happier race of beings.

But the most important branch of civilization, and which has most strenuously been extolled, by the zealous and pious fathers of the Roman Church, is the introduction of the Christian faith. It was truly a sight that might well inspire horror, to behold these savages, stumbling among the dark mountains of paganism, and guilty of the most horrible ignorance of religion. It is true, they neither stole nor defrauded, they were sober, frugal, continent, and faithful to their word; but though they acted right habitually, it was all in vain, unless they acted so from precept. The newcomers therefore used every method, to induce them to embrace and practice the true religion— except that of setting them the example.

But not withstanding all these complicated labours for their good, such was the unparalleled obstinacy of these stubborn wretches, that they ungratefully refused, to acknowledge the strangers as their bene-factors, and persisted in disbelieving the doctrines they endeavoured to inculcate; most insolently alleging, that from their conduct, the advocates of Christianity did not seem to believe in it themselves. Was not this too much for human patience? would not one suppose, that the foreign emigrants from Europe, provoked at their incredu-lity and discouraged by their stiff-necked obstinacy, would forever have abandoned their shores, and consigned them to their original ignorance and misery? But no—so zealous were they to effect the temporal comfort and eternal salvation of these pagan infidels, that they even proceeded from the milder means of persuasion, to the more painful and troublesome one of persecution—let loose among them whole troops of fiery monks and furious blood-hounds—purified them by fire and sword, by stake and faggot;[1] in consequence of which indefatigable measures, the cause of Christian love and charity were so rapidly advanced, that in a very few years, not one fifth of the number of unbelievers existed in South America, that were found there at the time of its discovery.

Nor did the other methods of civilization remain unenforced. The Indians improved daily and wonderfully by their intercourse with the whites. They took to drinking rum, and making bargains. They learned to cheat, to lie, to swear, to gamble, to quarrel, to cut each other's throats—in short, to excel in all the accomplishments that had originally marked the superiority of their Christian visitors. And such a surprising aptitude have they shown for these acquirements, that there is very little doubt that in a century more, provided they survive so long the irresistible effects of civilization, they will equal in knowledge, refinement, knavery, and debauchery, the most enlightened, civilized and orthodox nations of Europe.

What stronger right need the European settlers advance to the country than this? Have not whole nations of uninformed savages been made acquainted with a thousand imperious wants and indispensable comforts of which they were before wholly ignorant? Have they not been literally hunted and smoked out of the dens and lurking places of ignorance and infidelity, and absolutely scourged into the right path? Have not the temporal things, the vain baubles and filthy lucre of this world, which were too apt to engage their worldly and selfish thoughts, been benevolently taken from them; and have they not in lieu thereof, been taught to set their affections on things above? And finally, to use the words of a reverend Spanish father, in a letter to his superior in Spain—"Can any one have the presumption to say, that these savage Pagans, have yielded anything more than an inconsiderable recompense to their benefactors; in surrendering to them a little pitiful tract of this dirty sublunary planet, in exchange for a glorious inheritance in the kingdom of Heaven!"

Here then are three complete and undeniable sources of right established, any one of which was more than ample to establish a

---

1   *faggot*   Bundle of sticks for kindling.

property in the newly discovered regions of America. Now, so it has happened in certain parts of this delightful quarter of the globe, that the right of discovery has been so strenuously asserted—the influence of cultivation so industriously extended, and the progress of salvation and civilization so zealously prosecuted, that, what with their attendant wars, persecutions, oppressions, diseases, and other partial evils that often hang on the skirts of great benefits—the savage aborigines have, somehow or other, been utterly annihilated—and this all at once brings me to a fourth right, which is worth all the others put together. For the original claimants to the soil being all dead and buried, and no one remaining to inherit or dispute the soil, the Spaniards as the next immediate occupants entered upon the possession, as clearly as the hang-man succeeds to the clothes of the malefactor—and as they have Blackstone,[1] and all the learned expounders of the law on their side, they may set all actions of ejectment at defiance—and this last right may be entitled, the right by extermination, or in other words, the right by gunpowder.

But lest any scruples of conscience should remain on this head, and to settle the question of right forever, his holiness Pope Alexander VI, issued one of those mighty bulls,[2] which bear down reason, argument and everything before them; by which he generously granted the newly discovered quarter of the globe, to the Spaniards and Portuguese; who, thus having law and gospel on their side, and being inflamed with great spiritual zeal, showed the Pagan savages neither favour nor affection, but prosecuted the work of discovery, colonization, civilization, and extermination, with ten times more fury than ever.

Thus were the European worthies who first discovered America, clearly entitled to the soil; and not only entitled to the soil, but likewise to the eternal thanks of these infidel savages, for having come so far, endured so many perils by sea and land, and taken such unwearied pains, for no other purpose under heaven but to improve

---

1   *Blackstone*   English jurist William Blackstone, whose *Commentaries on the Laws of England* (1765–70) was immensely influential on the theory and practice of common law in Britain and the United States; in Book Two, Chapter One, Blackstone writes that "The most universal and effectual way of abandoning property, is by the death of the occupant. ... For, naturally speaking, the instant a man ceases to be, he ceases to have any dominion."

2   *Pope Alexander VI*   Pope from 1492 to 1503;   *bulls*   Papal mandates.

their forlorn, uncivilized and heathenish condition—for having made them acquainted with the comforts of life, such as gin, rum, brandy, and the small-pox; for having introduced among them the light of religion, and finally—for having hurried them out of the world, to enjoy its reward!

But as argument is never so well understood by us selfish mortals, as when it comes home to ourselves, and as I am particularly anxious that this question should be put to rest forever, I will suppose a parallel case, by way of arousing the candid attention of my readers.

Let us suppose then, that the inhabitants of the moon, by astonishing advancement in science, and by profound insight into that ineffable lunar philosophy, the mere flickerings of which, have of late years, dazzled the feeble optics, and addled the shallow brains of the good people of our globe—let us suppose, I say, that the inhabitants of the moon, by these means, had arrived at such a command of their *energies*, such an enviable state of *perfectibility*, as to control the elements, and navigate the boundless regions of space. Let us suppose a roving crew of these soaring philosophers, in the course of an aerial voyage of discovery among the stars, should chance to alight upon this outlandish planet.

And here I beg my readers will not have the impertinence to smile, as is too frequently the fault of volatile readers, when perusing the grave speculations of philosophers. I am far from indulging in any sportive vein at present, nor is the supposition I have been making so wild as many may deem it. It has long been a very serious and anxious question with me, and many a time, and oft, in the course of my overwhelming cares and contrivances for the welfare and protection of this my native planet, have I lain awake whole nights, debating in my mind whether it was most probable we should first discover and civilize the moon, or the moon discover and civilize our globe. Neither would the prodigy of sailing in the air or cruising among the stars be a whit more astonishing and incomprehensible to us, than was the European mystery of navigating floating castles through the world of waters, to the simple savages. We have already discovered the art of coasting along the aerial shores of our planet, by means of balloons, as the savages had, of venturing along their sea coasts in canoes; and the disparity between the former, and the aerial vehicles of the philosophers from the moon, might not be greater, than that, between the bark canoes of the savages, and the mighty ships of their discoverers. I might here pursue an endless chain of very curious, profound and unprofitable speculations; but as they would be unimportant to my subject, I abandon them to my reader, particularly if he be a philosopher, as matters well worthy his attentive consideration.

To return then to my supposition—let us suppose that the aerial visitants I have mentioned, possessed of vastly superior knowledge to ourselves; that is to say, possessed of superior knowledge in the art of extermination—riding on Hippogriffs, defended with impenetrable armour—armed with concentrated sun beams, and provided with vast engines, to hurl enormous moon stones: in short, let us suppose them, if our vanity will permit the supposition, as superior to us in knowledge, and consequently in power, as the Europeans were to the Indians, when they first discovered them. All this is very possible, it is only our self-sufficiency, that makes us think otherwise; and I warrant the poor savages, before they had any knowledge of the white men, armed in all the terrors of glittering steel and tremendous gunpowder, were as perfectly convinced that they themselves, were the wisest, the most virtuous, powerful and perfect of created beings, as are, at this present moment, the lordly inhabitants of old England, the volatile populace of France, or even the self-satisfied citizens of this most enlightened republic.

Let us suppose, moreover, that the aerial voyagers, finding this planet to be nothing but a howling wilderness, inhabited by us, poor savages and wild beasts, shall take formal possession of it, in the name of his most gracious and philosophic excellency, the man in the moon. Finding however, that their numbers are incompetent to hold it in complete subjection, on account of the ferocious barbarity of its inhabitants; they shall take our worthy President, the King of England, the Emperor of Haiti, the mighty little Bonaparte, and the great King of Bantam,[1] and returning to their native planet, shall carry them to court, as were the Indian chiefs led about as spectacles in the courts of Europe.

---

1   *Emperor of Haiti*   Following the Haitian Revolution (1791–1804), the First Empire of Haiti was ruled by Emperor Jean-Jacques Dessalines until his assassination in 1806. By the time Irving was writing the *History*, however, Haiti was a republic; *Bantam*   Sultanate in present-day Indonesia.

Then making such obeisance as the etiquette of the court requires, they shall address the puissant man in the moon, in, as near as I can conjecture, the following terms:

"Most serene and mighty Potentate, whose dominions extend as far as eye can reach, who rideth on the Great Bear,[1] useth the sun as a looking glass and maintaineth unrivalled control over tides, madmen, and sea-crabs. We thy liege subjects have just returned from a voyage of discovery, in the course of which we have landed and taken possession of that obscure little scurvy planet, which thou beholdest rolling at a distance. The five uncouth monsters, which we have brought into this august presence, were once very important chiefs among their fellow savages; for the inhabitants of the newly discovered globe are totally destitute of the common attributes of humanity, inasmuch as they carry their heads upon their shoulders, instead of under their arms—have two eyes instead of one—are utterly destitute of tails, and of a variety of unseemly complexions, particularly of horrible whiteness—whereas all the inhabitants of the moon are pea green!

"We have moreover found these miserable savages sunk into a state of the utmost ignorance and depravity, every man shamelessly living with his own wife, and rearing his own children, instead of indulging in that community of wives, enjoined by the law of nature, as expounded by the philosophers of the moon. In a word they have scarcely a gleam of true philosophy among them, but are, in fact, utter heretics, ignoramuses and barbarians. Taking compassion therefore on the sad condition of these sublunary wretches, we have endeavoured, while we remained on their planet, to introduce among them the light of reason—and the comforts of the moon. We have treated them to mouthfuls of moonshine and draughts of nitrous oxide, which they swallowed with incredible voracity, particularly the females; and we have likewise endeavoured to instil into them the precepts of lunar Philosophy. We have insisted upon their renouncing the contemptable shackles of religion and common sense, and adoring the profound, omnipotent, and all perfect energy, and the ecstatic, immutable, immovable perfection. But such was the unparalleled obstinacy of these wretched savages, that they persisted in cleaving to their wives and adhering to their

---

1   *Great Bear*   Constellation also colloquially known as the Big Dipper.

religion, and absolutely set at naught the sublime doctrines of the moon—nay, among other abominable heresies they even went so far as blasphemously to declare, that this ineffable planet was made of nothing more nor less than green cheese!"

At these words, the great man in the moon (being a very profound philosopher) shall fall into a terrible passion, and possessing equal authority over things that do not belong to him, as did whilome[1] his holiness the Pope, shall forthwith issue a formidable bull, specifying "That—whereas a certain crew of Lunatics[2] have lately discovered and taken possession of that little dirty planet, called *the earth*—and that whereas it is inhabited by none but a race of two legged animals, that carry their heads on their shoulders instead of under their arms; cannot talk the Lunatic language; have two eyes instead of one; are destitute of tails, and of a horrible whiteness, instead of pea green— therefore and for a variety of other excellent reasons—they are considered incapable of possessing any property in the planet they infest, and the right and title to it are confirmed to its original discoverers. And furthermore, the colonists who are now about to depart to the aforesaid planet, are authorized and commanded to use every means to convert these infidel savages from the darkness of Christianity, and make them thorough and absolute Lunatics."

In consequence of this benevolent bull, our philosophic benefactors go to work with hearty zeal. They seize upon our fertile territories, scourge us from our rightful possessions, relieve us from our wives, and when we are unreasonable enough to complain, they will turn upon us and say—miserable barbarians! ungrateful wretches! Have we not come thousands of miles to improve your worthless planet—have we not fed you with moon shine—have we not intoxicated you with nitrous oxide—does not our moon give you light every night—and have you the baseness to murmur, when we claim a pitiful return for all these benefits? But finding that we not only persist in absolute contempt to their reasoning and disbelief in their philosophy, but even go so far as daringly to defend our property, their patience shall be exhausted, and they shall resort to their superior powers of argument—hunt us with hypogriffs, transfix us with concentrated

---

1   *whilome*   Once; formerly.
2   *Lunatics*   Punning on the Latin word for moon, "Luna." (In its original use, the word "lunatic" referenced those whose insanity was affected by the lunar cycles.)

sun-beams, demolish our cities with moonstones; until having by main force, converted us to the true faith, they shall graciously permit us to exist in the torrid deserts of Arabia, or the frozen regions of Lapland,[1] there to enjoy the blessings of civilization and the charms of lunar philosophy—in much the same manner as the reformed and enlightened savages of this country, are kindly suffered to inhabit the inhospitable forests of the north, or the impenetrable wilderness of South America.

Thus have I clearly proved, and I hope strikingly illustrated, the right of the early colonists to the possession of this country—and thus is this gigantic question, completely knocked in the head—so having manfully surmounted all obstacles, and subdued all opposition, what remains but that I should forthwith conduct my impatient and wayworn readers, into the renowned city, which we have so long been in a manner besieging. But hold, before I proceed another step, I must pause to take breath and recover from the excessive fatigue I have undergone, in preparing to begin this most accurate of histories. And in this I do but imitate the example of the celebrated Hans Von Dunderbottom, who took a start of three miles for the purpose of jumping over a hill, but having been himself out of breath by the time he reached the foot, sat himself quietly down for a few moments to blow, and then walked over it at his leisure.

—1809

---

1 *Lapland* Northernmost region of Finland.

from THE SKETCH BOOK OF
GEOFFREY CRAYON, GENT.

The Wife[1]

The treasures of the deep are not so precious
As are the concealed comforts of a man
Lock'd up in woman's love. I scent the air
Of blessings, when I come but near the house.
What a delicious breath marriage sends forth—
The violet bed's not sweeter![2]

MIDDLETON

I have often had occasion to remark the fortitude with which women sustain the most overwhelming reverses of fortune. Those disasters which break down the spirit of a man, and prostrate him in the dust, seem to call forth all the energies of the softer sex, and give such intrepidity and elevation to their character, that at times it approaches to sublimity. Nothing can be more touching than to behold a soft and tender female, who had been all weakness and dependence, and alive to every trivial roughness while treading the prosperous paths of life, suddenly rising in mental force, to be the comforter and supporter of her husband, under misfortune, and abiding, with unshrinking firmness, the bitterest blasts of adversity.

As the vine which has long twined its graceful foliage around the oak, and been lifted by it into sunshine, will, when the hardy plant is rifted by the thunderbolt, cling round it with its caressing tendrils, and bind up its shattered boughs; so is it beautifully ordered by Providence, that woman, who is the mere dependant and ornament of man in his happier hours, should be his stay and solace when smitten with sudden calamity, winding herself into the rugged recesses of his nature, tenderly supporting the drooping head, and binding up the broken heart.

I was once congratulating a friend, who had around him a blooming family, knit together in the strongest affection. "I can wish you no better lot," said he, with enthusiasm, "than to have a wife and

---

1   Irving placed this tale immediately before "Rip Van Winkle" in the first American edition of *The Sketch Book* (1819).

2   *The treasures ... not sweeter!*   See Thomas Middleton's Jacobean play *Women Beware Women* 3.1 (1657).

children—if you are prosperous, there they are to share your prosperity; if otherwise, there they are to comfort you." And, indeed, I have observed that married men falling into misfortune, are more apt to retrieve their situation in the world than single men; partly because they are more stimulated to exertion by the necessities of the helpless and beloved beings who depend upon them for subsistence; but chiefly because their spirits are soothed and relieved by domestic endearments, and their self-respect kept alive by finding, that though all abroad is darkness and humiliation, yet there is still a little world of love, of which they are monarchs. Whereas a single man is apt to run to waste and self neglect; to fancy himself lonely and abandoned, and his heart to fall to ruin like some deserted mansion, for want of an inhabitant.

These observations call to mind a little domestic story, of which I was once a witness. My intimate friend, Leslie, had married a beautiful and accomplished girl, who had been brought up in the midst of fashionable life. She had, it is true, no fortune, but that of my friend was ample; and he delighted in the anticipation of indulging her in every elegant pursuit, and administering to those delicate tastes and fancies, that spread a kind of witchery about the sex. "Her life," said he, "shall be like a fairy tale."

The very difference in their characters produced an harmonious combination: he was of a romantic, and somewhat serious, cast; she was all life and gladness. I have often noticed the mute rapture with which he would gaze upon her in company, of which her sprightly powers made her the delight; and how, in the midst of applause, her eye would still turn to him, as if there alone she sought favour and acceptance. When leaning on his arm, her slender form contrasted finely with his tall, manly person. The fond confiding air with which she looked up to him, seemed to call forth a flush of triumphant pride and cherishing tenderness, as if he doted on his lovely burden for its very helplessness. Never did a couple set forward on the flowery path of early and well-suited marriage with a fairer prospect of felicity.

It was the mishap of my friend, however, to have embarked his fortune in large speculations; and he had not been married many months, when, by a succession of sudden disasters, it was swept from him, and he found himself reduced almost to penury. For a time he kept his situation to himself, and went about with a haggard countenance, and a breaking heart. His life was but a protracted agony; and what rendered it more insupportable, was the necessity of keeping up a smile in the presence of his wife; for he could not bring himself to overwhelm her with the news. She saw, however, with the quick eyes of affection, that all was not well with him. She marked his altered looks and stifled sighs, and was not to be deceived by his sickly and vapid attempts at cheerfulness. She tasked all her sprightly powers and tender blandishments to win him back to happiness; but she only drove the arrow deeper into his soul. The more he saw cause to love her, the more torturing was the thought that he was soon to make her wretched. A little while, thought he, and the smile will vanish from that cheek—the song will die away from those lips—the lustre of those eyes will be quenched with sorrow; and the happy heart which now beats lightly in that bosom, will be weighed down, like mine, by the cares and miseries of the world.

At length he came to me one day, and related his whole situation in a tone of the deepest despair. When I had heard him through, I inquired, "does your wife know all this?" At the question he burst into an agony of tears. "For God's sake!" cried he, "if you have any pity on me, don't mention my wife; it is the thought of her that drives me almost to madness!"

"And why not?" said I. "She must know it sooner or later: you cannot keep it long from her, and the intelligence may break upon her in a more startling manner, than if imparted by yourself; for the accents of those we love soften the harshest tidings. Besides, you are depriving yourself of the comforts of her sympathy; and not merely that, but also endangering the only bond that can keep hearts together—an unreserved community of thought and feeling. She will soon perceive that something is secretly preying upon your mind; and true love will not brook reserve, but feels undervalued and outraged, when even the sorrows of those it loves are concealed from it."

"Oh, but, my friend! to think what a blow I am to give to all her future prospects—how I am to strike her very soul to the earth, by telling her that her husband is a beggar! that she is to forego all the elegancies of life—all the pleasures of society—to shrink with me into indigence and obscurity! To tell her that I have dragged her down from the sphere in which she might have continued to move in constant brightness—the light of every eye—the admiration of every heart! How can she bear poverty? she has been brought up in all the refinements of opulence. How can she bear neglect? she has been the idol of society. Oh, it will break her heart, it will break her heart!"

I saw his grief was eloquent, and I let it have its flow; for sorrow relieves itself by words. When his paroxysm had subsided, and he had relapsed into moody silence, I resumed the subject gently, and urged him to break his situation at once to his wife. He shook his head mournfully, but positively.

"But how are you to keep it from her? It is necessary she should know it, that you may take the steps proper to the alteration of your circumstances. You must change your style of living—nay," observing a pang to pass across his countenance, "don't let that afflict you. I am sure you have never placed your happiness in outward show—you have yet friends, warm friends, who will not think the worse of you for being less splendidly lodged: and surely it does not require a palace to be happy with Mary—"

"I could be happy with her," cried he convulsively, "in a hovel! I could go down with her into poverty and the dust! I could—I could—God bless her! God bless her!" cried he, bursting into a transport of grief and tenderness.

"And believe me, my friend," said I, stepping up, and grasping him warmly by the hand, "believe me, she can be the same with you. Aye, more: it will be a source of pride and triumph to her—it will call forth all the latent energies and fervent sympathies of her nature; for she will rejoice to prove that she loves you for yourself. There is in every true woman's heart a spark of heavenly fire, which lies dormant in the broad daylight of prosperity; but which kindles up, and beams and blazes in the dark hour of adversity. No man knows what the wife of his bosom is—no man knows what a ministering angel she is—until he has gone with her through the fiery trials of this world."

There was something in the earnestness of my manner, and the figurative style of my language, that caught the excited imagination of Leslie. I knew the auditor I had to deal with; and following up the impression I had made, I finished by persuading him to go home and unburden his sad heart to his wife.

I must confess, notwithstanding all I had said, I felt some little solicitude for the result. Who can calculate on the fortitude of one whose whole life has been a round of pleasures? Her gay spirits might revolt at the dark, downward path of low humility, suddenly pointed out before her, and might cling to the sunny regions in which they had hitherto revelled. Besides, ruin in fashionable life is accompanied by so many galling mortifications, to which, in other ranks, it is a stranger. In short, I could not meet Leslie, the next morning, without trepidation. He had made the disclosure.

"And how did she bear it?"

"Like an angel! It seemed rather to be a relief to her mind, for she threw her arms around my neck, and asked if this was all that had lately made me unhappy—but, poor girl," added he, "she cannot realize the change we must undergo. She has no idea of poverty but in the abstract: she has only read of it in poetry, where it is allied to love. She feels as yet no privation: she experiences no want of accustomed conveniences or elegancies. When we come practically to experience its sordid cares, its paltry wants, its petty humiliations—then will be the real trial."

"But," said I, "now that you have got over the severest task, that of breaking it to her, the sooner you let the world into the secret the better. The disclosure may be mortifying; but then it is a single misery, and soon over; whereas you otherwise suffer it, in anticipation, every hour in the day. It is not poverty, so much as pretence, that harasses a ruined man—the struggle between a proud mind and an empty purse—the keeping up a hollow show that must soon come to an end. Have the courage to appear poor, and you disarm poverty of its sharpest sting." On this point I found Leslie perfectly prepared. He had no false pride himself, and as to his wife, she was only anxious to conform to their altered fortunes.

Some days afterwards he called upon me in the evening. He had disposed of his dwelling house, and taken a small cottage in the country, a few miles from town. He had been busied all day in sending out furniture. The new establishment required few articles, and those of the simplest kind. All the splendid furniture of his late residence had been sold, excepting his wife's harp. That, he said, was too closely associated with the idea of herself; it belonged to the little story of their loves; for some of the sweetest moments of their courtship were those when he had leaned over that instrument, and listened to the melting tones of her voice. I could not but smile at this instance of romantic gallantry in a doting husband.

He was now going out to the cottage, where his wife had been all day, superintending its arrangement. My feelings had become strongly interested in the progress of this family story, and as it was a fine evening, I offered to accompany him.

He was wearied with the fatigues of the day, and as we walked out, fell into a fit of gloomy musing.

"Poor Mary!" at length broke, with a heavy sigh, from his lips.

"And what of her," asked I, "has any thing happened to her?"

"What," said he, darting an impatient glance, "is it nothing to be reduced to this paltry situation—to be caged in a miserable cottage—to be obliged to toil almost in the menial concerns of her wretched habitation?"

"Has she then repined at the change?"

"Repined! she has been nothing but sweetness and good humour. Indeed, she seems in better spirits than I have ever known her; she has been to me all love, and tenderness, and comfort!"

"Admirable girl!" exclaimed I. "You call yourself poor, my friend; you never were so rich—you never knew the boundless treasures of excellence you possessed in that woman."

"Oh, but my friend, if this first meeting at the cottage were over, I think I could then be comfortable. But this is her first day of real experience. She has been introduced into a humble dwelling—she has been employed all day in arranging its miserable equipments—she has for the first time known the fatigues of domestic employment—she has for the first time looked around her on a home destitute of everything elegant, and almost convenient;[1] and may now be sitting down, exhausted and spiritless, brooding over a prospect of future poverty."

There was a degree of probability in this picture that I could not gainsay, so we walked on in silence.

After turning from the main road, up a narrow lane, so thickly shaded by forest trees, as to give it a complete air of seclusion, we came in sight of the cottage. It was humble enough in its appearance for the most pastoral poet; and yet it had a pleasing rural look. A wild vine had overrun one end with a profusion of foliage; a few trees

---

1 *destitute of ... convenient* Lacking not only in things of elegance, but also in everyday conveniences.

threw their branches gracefully over it; and I observed several pots of flowers tastefully disposed about the door, and on the grass plot in front. A small wicket gate opened upon a footpath that wound through some shrubbery to the door. Just as we approached, we heard the sound of music—Leslie grasped my arm; we paused and listened. It was Mary's voice, in a style of the most touching simplicity, singing a little air[1] of which her husband was peculiarly fond.

I felt Leslie's hand tremble on my arm. He stepped forward, to hear more distinctly. His step made a noise on the gravel walk. A bright beautiful face glanced out at the window, and vanished—a light footstep was heard—and Mary came tripping forth to meet us. She was in a pretty rural dress of white; a few wild flowers were twisted in her fine hair; a fresh bloom was on her cheek; her whole countenance beamed with smiles—I had never seen her look so lovely.

"My dear George," cried she, "I am so glad you are come; I've been watching and watching for you; and running down the lane, and looking out for you. I've set out a table under a beautiful tree behind the cottage; and I've been gathering some of the most delicious strawberries, for I know you are fond of them—and we have such excellent cream—and every thing is so sweet and still here—Oh!" said she, putting her arm within his, and looking up brightly in his face, "Oh, we shall be so snug!"

Poor Leslie was overcome.—He caught her to his bosom—he folded his arms around her—he kissed her again and again—he could not speak, but the tears gushed into his eyes. And he has often assured me, that though the world has since gone prosperously with him, and his life has been a happy one, yet never has he experienced a moment of such unutterable felicity.

—1819

---

1   *air* Style of song, often played on the piano at polite gatherings.

Rip Van Winkle

[The following Tale was found among the papers of the late Diedrich Knickerbocker, an old gentleman of New York, who was very curious in the Dutch history of the province,[1] and the manners of the descendants from its primitive settlers. His historical researches, however, did not lay so much among books, as among men; for the former are lamentably scanty on his favourite topics; whereas he found the old burghers,[2] and still more, their wives, rich in that legendary lore, so invaluable to true history. Whenever, therefore, he happened upon a genuine Dutch family, snugly shut up in its low-roofed farm house, under a spreading sycamore, he looked upon it as a little clasped volume of black-letter,[3] and studied it with the zeal of a bookworm.

The result of all these researches was a history of the province, during the reign of the Dutch governors, which he published some years since. There have been various opinions as to the literary character of his work, and, to tell the truth, it is not a whit better than it should be. Its chief merit is its scrupulous accuracy, which, indeed, was a little questioned, on its first appearance, but has since been completely established; and it is now admitted into all historical collections, as a book of unquestionable authority.

The old gentleman died shortly after the publication of his work, and now, that he is dead and gone, it cannot do much harm to his memory, to say, that his time might have been much better employed in weightier labours. He, however, was apt to ride his hobby his own way; and though it did now and then kick up the dust a little in the eyes of his neighbours, and grieve the spirit of some friends, for whom he felt the truest deference and affection; yet his errors and follies are remembered

---

1   *Diedrich Knickerbocker* Allusion to the fictional author of Irving's parody *History of New York* (1809); *curious* Interested; *Dutch history ... province* In the early to mid-seventeenth century, the Dutch Republic colonized land on the east coast of North America, calling this territory New Netherland. The territory was ceded to Britain in 1664 and renamed the Province of New York, with the town of New Amsterdam also being named New York.
2   *burghers* Citizens.
3   *black-letter* Gothic-style typeface used in early printed material; black-letter books were regarded as valuable and important, and therefore often fitted with clasps and locks.

"more in sorrow than in anger,"[1] and it begins to be suspected, that he never intended to injure or offend. But however his memory may be appreciated by critics, it is still held dear among many folk, whose good opinion is well worth having; particularly certain biscuit bakers, who have gone so far as to imprint his likeness on their new year cakes, and have thus given him a chance for immortality, almost equal to being stamped on a Waterloo medal, or a Queen Anne's farthing.[2]]

Rip Van Winkle
A Posthumous Writing of Diedrich Knickerbocker

> By Woden, God of Saxons,
> From whence comes Wensday, that is Wodensday,
> Truth is a thing that ever I will keep
> Unto thylke day in which I creep into
> My sepulchre—
> CARTWRIGHT[3]

Whoever has made a voyage up the Hudson[4] must remember the Kaatskill mountains. They are a dismembered branch of the great Appalachian family, and are seen away to the west of the river, swelling up to a noble height, and lording it over the surrounding country. Every change of season, every change of weather, indeed, every hour of the day, produces some change in the magical hues and shapes of these mountains, and they are regarded by all the good wives, far and near, as perfect barometers. When the weather is fair

---

1   [Irving's note]   Vide the excellent discourse of G.C. Verplanck, Esq. before the New-York Historical Society. [Gulian C. Verplanck was a politician, writer, and founder of the New York Historical Society, who had disparaged Irving's parodic *History of New York*; also see Horatio's description of the King's ghost in Shakespeare's *Hamlet* 1.2.232: "A countenance more in sorrow than in anger."]

2   *Waterloo medal ... Anne's farthing*   Waterloo medals were widely distributed to those who fought in the battles leading up to the defeat of Napoleon in 1815; Queen Anne's farthings, small coins worth a quarter of a penny, were only accidentally circulated after the Queen's death in 1714, and then incorrectly believed to be highly valuable.

3   *By Woden ... CARTWRIGHT*   Excerpt from William Cartwright's 1635 play *The Ordinary* (3.1.1050–54); lines spoken by a pedantic antiquarian named Moth;   *Woden*   Foremost god in Norse mythology.

4   *Hudson*   Hudson River, which runs through what is now New York State; the river was named after English explorer Henry Hudson, who sailed for the Dutch East India Company in the early seventeenth century.

and settled, they are clothed in blue and purple, and print their bold outlines on the clear evening sky; but sometimes, when the rest of the landscape is cloudless, they will gather a hood of gray vapours about their summits, which, in the last rays of the setting sun, will glow and light up like a crown of glory.

At the foot of these fairy mountains, the voyager may have descried[1] the light smoke curling up from a village, whose shingle roofs gleam among the trees, just where the blue tints of the upland melt away into the fresh green of the nearer landscape. It is a little village of great antiquity, having been founded by some of the Dutch colonists, in the early times of the province, just about the beginning of the government of the good Peter Stuyvesant[2] (may he rest in peace!), and there were some of the houses of the original settlers standing within a few years, with lattice windows, gable fronts surmounted with weathercocks, and built of small yellow bricks brought from Holland.

In that same village, and in one of these very houses (which, to tell the precise truth, was sadly time-worn and weather-beaten), there lived many years since, while the country was yet a province of Great Britain, a simple, good-natured fellow, of the name of Rip Van Winkle. He was a descendant of the Van Winkles who figured so gallantly in the chivalrous days of Peter Stuyvesant, and accompanied him to the siege of Fort Christina.[3] He inherited, however, but little of the martial character of his ancestors. I have observed that he was a simple, good-natured man; he was moreover a kind neighbour, and an obedient, henpecked husband. Indeed, to the latter circumstance might be owing that meekness of spirit which gained him such universal popularity; for those men are most apt to be obsequious and conciliating abroad, who are under the discipline of shrews[4] at home. Their tempers, doubtless, are rendered pliant and malleable in the fiery furnace of domestic tribulation, and a curtain lecture[5] is worth

---

1   *descried*   Discerned; caught sight of.

2   *Peter Stuyvesant*   Last director-general of the colony of New Netherland, from 1647 until 1664, when he ceded the territory to the English.

3   *Fort Christina*   Swedish colony in what is now the state of Delaware, where Swedish troops were defeated by Stuyvesant in 1655, effectively ending Swedish colonialism in North America.

4   *shrews*   Derogatory term for controlling or nagging women.

5   *curtain lecture*   Archaic term describing the scolding by a wife of her husband, with the further implication that she denies his sexual advances, while behind the curtains of their bed.

all the sermons in the world for teaching the virtues of patience and long suffering. A termagant[1] wife may, therefore, in some respects, be considered a tolerable blessing; and if so, Rip Van Winkle was thrice blessed.

Certain it is, that he was a great favourite among all the good wives of the village, who, as usual with the amiable sex, took his part in all family squabbles, and never failed, whenever they talked those matters over in their evening gossippings, to lay all the blame on Dame Van Winkle. The children of the village, too, would shout with joy whenever he approached. He assisted at their sports, made their playthings, taught them to fly kites and shoot marbles, and told them long stories of ghosts, witches, and Indians. Whenever he went dodging about the village, he was surrounded by a troop of them, hanging on his skirts, clambering on his back, and playing a thousand tricks on him with impunity; and not a dog would bark at him throughout the neighbourhood.

The great error in Rip's composition was an insuperable aversion to all kinds of profitable labour.[2] It could not be for the want of assiduity or perseverance; for he would sit on a wet rock, with a rod as long and heavy as a Tartar's lance, and fish all day without a murmur, even though he should not be encouraged by a single nibble. He would carry a fowling piece[3] on his shoulder for hours together, trudging through woods and swamps, and up hill and down dale, to shoot a few squirrels or wild pigeons. He would never even refuse to assist a neighbour in the roughest toil, and was a foremost man at all country frolics for husking Indian corn, or building stone fences; the women of the village, too, used to employ him to run their errands, and to do such little odd jobs as their less obliging husbands would not do for them—in a word, Rip was ready to attend to anybody's business but his own; but as to doing family duty, and keeping his farm in order, it was impossible.

In fact, he declared it was no use to work on his farm; it was the most pestilent little piece of ground in the whole country; everything about it went wrong, and would go wrong, in spite of him. His fences

---

1   *termagant* Bad-tempered; shrewish.

2   *The great error ... profitable labour* I.e., Rip's greatest character flaw was his constant distaste for doing useful work.

3   *fowling piece* Small gun for hunting wild birds.

were continually falling to pieces; his cow would either go astray, or get among the cabbages; weeds were sure to grow quicker in his fields than anywhere else; the rain always made a point of setting in just as he had some outdoor work to do. So that though his patrimonial estate had dwindled away under his management, acre by acre, until there was little more left than a mere patch of Indian corn and potatoes, yet it was the worst conditioned farm in the neighbourhood.

His children, too, were as ragged and wild as if they belonged to nobody. His son Rip, an urchin begotten in his own likeness, promised to inherit the habits, with the old clothes of his father. He was generally seen trooping like a colt at his mother's heels, equipped in a pair of his father's cast-off galligaskins,[1] which he had much ado to hold up with one hand, as a fine lady does her train in bad weather.

Rip Van Winkle, however, was one of those happy mortals, of foolish, well-oiled dispositions, who take the world easy, eat white bread or brown, whichever can be got with least thought or trouble, and would rather starve on a penny than work for a pound. If left to himself, he would have whistled life away in perfect contentment; but his wife kept continually dinning in his ears about his idleness, his carelessness, and the ruin he was bringing on his family. Morning, noon, and night, her tongue was incessantly going, and everything he said or did was sure to produce a torrent of household eloquence. Rip had but one way of replying to all lectures of the kind, and that, by frequent use, had grown into a habit. He shrugged his shoulders, shook his head, cast up his eyes, but said nothing. This, however, always provoked a fresh volley from his wife, so that he was fain to draw off his forces,[2] and take to the outside of the house—the only side which, in truth, belongs to a henpecked husband.

Rip's sole domestic adherent was his dog Wolf, who was as much henpecked as his master; for Dame Van Winkle regarded them as companions in idleness, and even looked upon Wolf with an evil eye, as the cause of his master's so often going astray. True it is, in all points of spirit befitting an honourable dog, he was as courageous an animal as ever scoured the woods—but what courage can withstand the ever-during and all-besetting terrors of a woman's tongue? The

---

1 *galligaskins* Loose-fitting style of breeches or trousers.
2 *fain to ... his forces* I.e., inclined to withdraw from the interaction.

moment Wolf entered the house, his crest fell, his tail drooped to the ground, or curled between his legs, he sneaked about with a gallows air,[1] casting many a sidelong glance at Dame Van Winkle, and at the least flourish of a broomstick or ladle, would fly to the door with yelping precipitation.

Times grew worse and worse with Rip Van Winkle as years of matrimony rolled on; a tart temper never mellows with age, and a sharp tongue is the only edge tool that grows keener[2] by constant use. For a long while he used to console himself, when driven from home, by frequenting a kind of perpetual club of the sages, philosophers, and other idle personages of the village, that held its sessions on a bench before a small inn, designated by a rubicund portrait of his majesty George the Third.[3] Here they used to sit in the shade, of a long lazy summer's day, talk listlessly over village gossip, or tell endless sleepy stories about nothing. But it would have been worth any statesman's money to have heard the profound discussions that sometimes took place, when by chance an old newspaper fell into their hands, from some passing traveller. How solemnly they would listen to the contents, as drawled out by Derrick Van Bummel, the schoolmaster, a dapper, learned little man, who was not to be daunted by the most gigantic word in the dictionary; and how sagely they would deliberate upon public events some months after they had taken place.

The opinions of this junto[4] were completely controlled by Nicholas Vedder, a patriarch of the village, and landlord of the inn, at the door of which he took his seat from morning till night, just moving sufficiently to avoid the sun, and keep in the shade of a large tree; so that the neighbours could tell the hour by his movements as accurately as by a sun dial. It is true, he was rarely heard to speak, but smoked his pipe incessantly. His adherents, however (for every great man has his adherents), perfectly understood him, and knew how to gather his opinions. When anything that was read or related displeased him, he was observed to smoke his pipe vehemently, and send forth short, frequent, and angry puffs; but when pleased, he

---

1   *gallows air*   Appearance of one ready for the gallows, to be hanged.
2   *keener*   Sharper.
3   *George the Third*   King of Great Britain from 1760 to 1820, and the last British monarch to rule over the Thirteen Colonies preceding the American Revolutionary War.
4   *junto*   Self-organized political committee or club.

would inhale the smoke slowly and tranquilly, and emit it in light and placid clouds, and sometimes taking the pipe from his mouth, and letting the fragrant vapour curl about his nose, would gravely nod his head in token of perfect approbation.

From even this stronghold the unlucky Rip was at length routed by his termagant wife, who would suddenly break in upon the tranquility of the assemblage, [and][1] call the members all to nought; nor was that august personage, Nicholas Vedder himself, sacred from the daring tongue of this terrible virago,[2] who charged him outright with encouraging her husband in habits of idleness.

Poor Rip was at last reduced almost to despair; and his only alternative to escape from the labour of the farm and the clamour of his wife, was to take gun in hand, and stroll away into the woods. Here he would sometimes seat himself at the foot of a tree, and share the contents of his wallet[3] with Wolf, with whom he sympathised as a fellow sufferer in persecution. "Poor Wolf," he would say, "thy mistress leads thee a dog's life of it; but never mind, my lad, while I live thou shalt never want a friend to stand by thee!" Wolf would wag his tail, look wistfully in his master's face, and if dogs can feel pity, I verily believe he reciprocated the sentiment with all his heart.

In a long ramble of the kind on a fine autumnal day, Rip had unconsciously scrambled to one of the highest parts of the Kaatskill mountains. He was after his favourite sport of squirrel shooting, and the still solitudes had echoed and re-echoed with the reports of his gun. Panting and fatigued, he threw himself, late in the afternoon, on a green knoll, covered with mountain herbage, that crowned the brow of a precipice. From an opening between the trees, he could overlook all the lower country for many a mile of rich woodland. He saw at a distance the lordly Hudson, far, far below him, moving on its silent but majestic course, the reflection of a purple cloud, or the sail of a lagging bark,[4] here and there sleeping on its glassy bosom, and at last losing itself in the blue highlands.

On the other side he looked down into a deep mountain glen, wild, lonely, and shagged, the bottom filled with fragments from the

---

1 *[and]* Irving added this word in later editions.
2 *virago* Fierce woman.
3 *wallet* Knapsack.
4 *bark* Small type of sailing boat.

impending cliffs, and scarcely lighted by the reflected rays of the setting sun. For some time Rip lay musing on this scene, evening was gradually advancing, the mountains began to throw their long blue shadows over the valleys, he saw that it would be dark long before he could reach the village, and he heaved a heavy sigh when he thought of encountering the terrors of Dame Van Winkle.

As he was about to descend, he heard a voice from a distance, hallooing, "Rip Van Winkle! Rip Van Winkle!" He looked around, but could see nothing but a crow winging its solitary flight across the mountain. He thought his fancy must have deceived him, and turned again to descend, when he heard the same cry ring through the still evening air; "Rip Van Winkle! Rip Van Winkle!"—at the same time Wolf bristled up his back, and giving a low growl, skulked to his master's side, looking fearfully down into the glen. Rip now felt a vague apprehension stealing over him; he looked anxiously in the same direction, and perceived a strange figure slowly toiling up the rocks, and bending under the weight of something he carried on his back. He was surprised to see any human being in this lonely and unfrequented place, but supposing it to be someone of the neighbourhood in need of his assistance, he hastened down to yield it.

On nearer approach, he was still more surprised at the singularity of the stranger's appearance. He was a short, square-built old fellow, with thick bushy hair, and a grizzled beard. His dress was of the antique Dutch fashion—a cloth jerkin[1] strapped round the waist—several pairs of breeches, the outer one of ample volume, decorated with rows of buttons down the sides, and bunches at the knees. He bore on his shoulder a stout keg, that seemed full of liquor, and made signs for Rip to approach and assist him with the load. Though rather shy and distrustful of this new acquaintance, Rip complied with his usual alacrity, and mutually relieving each other, they clambered up a narrow gully, apparently the dry bed of a mountain torrent. As they ascended, Rip every now and then heard long rolling peals, like distant thunder, that seemed to issue out of a deep ravine, or rather cleft between lofty rocks, toward which their rugged path conducted. He paused for an instant, but supposing it to be the muttering of one of

---

[1] *jerkin* Style of jacket fashionable during the seventeenth century, but no longer worn by the time of this story.

those transient thunder showers which often take place in mountain heights, he proceeded. Passing through the ravine, they came to a hollow, like a small amphitheatre, surrounded by perpendicular precipices, over the brinks of which impending trees shot their branches, so that you only caught glimpses of the azure sky, and the bright evening cloud. During the whole time, Rip and his companion had laboured on in silence; for though the former marvelled greatly what could be the object[1] of carrying a keg of liquor up this wild mountain, yet there was something strange and incomprehensible about the unknown, that inspired awe, and checked familiarity.[2]

On entering the amphitheatre, new objects of wonder presented themselves. On a level spot in the centre was a company of odd-looking personages playing at nine-pins.[3] They were dressed in a quaint, outlandish fashion: some wore short doublets,[4] others jerkins, with long knives in their belts, and most had enormous breeches, of similar style with that of the guide's. Their visages, too, were peculiar: one had a large head, broad face, and small piggish eyes; the face of another seemed to consist entirely of nose, and was surmounted by a white sugarloaf hat,[5] set off with a little red cockstail. They all had beards, of various shapes and colours. There was one who seemed to be the commander. He was a stout old gentleman, with a weather-beaten countenance; he wore a laced doublet, broad belt and hanger,[6] high crowned hat and feather, red stockings, and high-heeled shoes, with roses in them. The whole group reminded Rip of the figures in an old Flemish painting, in the parlour of Dominie[7] Van Schaick, the village parson, and which had been brought over from Holland at the time of the settlement.

What seemed particularly odd to Rip was that, though these folks were evidently amusing themselves, yet they maintained the gravest

---

1 *object* Purpose.

2 *checked familiarity* I.e., discouraged overt friendliness.

3 *nine-pins* Lawn game similar to modern-day bowling.

4 *doublets* Another form of male upper-body garment.

5 *sugarloaf hat* Tall, conical sort of hat, often associated with English Puritans and Pilgrims who settled the eastern Americas in the early 1600s.

6 *hanger* Short sword worn at the belt.

7 *old Flemish painting* Flemish art, hailing from Belgium and the Netherlands, developed its distinctive style during the late Renaissance; *Dominie* Title for a minister or parson, commonly used in the former Dutch colonies.

faces, the most mysterious silence, and were, withal, the most melancholy party of pleasure he had ever witnessed. Nothing interrupted the stillness of the scene, but the noise of the balls, which, whenever they were rolled, echoed along the mountains like rumbling peals of thunder.

As Rip and his companion approached them, they suddenly desisted from their play, and stared at him with such fixed statue-like gaze, and such strange, uncouth, lacklustre countenances, that his heart turned within him, and his knees smote together. His companion now emptied the contents of the keg into large flagons, and made signs to him to wait upon the company. He obeyed with fear and trembling;[1] they quaffed the liquor in profound silence, and then returned to their game.

By degrees, Rip's awe and apprehension subsided. He even ventured, when no eye was fixed upon him, to taste the beverage, which he found had much of the flavour of excellent Hollands.[2] He was naturally a thirsty soul, and was soon tempted to repeat the draught. One taste provoked another, and he reiterated his visits to the flagon so often, that at length his senses were overpowered, his eyes swam in his head, his head gradually declined, and he fell into a deep sleep.

On awakening, he found himself on the green knoll from whence he had first seen the old man of the glen. He rubbed his eyes—it was a bright sunny morning. The birds were hopping and twittering among the bushes, and the eagle was wheeling aloft, and breasting the pure mountain breeze. "Surely," thought Rip, "I have not slept here all night." He recalled the occurrences before he fell asleep. The strange man with the keg of liquor—the mountain ravine—the wild retreat among the rocks—the woebegone party at nine-pins—the flagon— "Oh! that flagon! that wicked flagon!" thought Rip—"what excuse shall I make to Dame Van Winkle?"

He looked round for his gun, but in place of the clean, well-oiled fowling piece, he found an old firelock lying by him, the barrel encrusted with rust, the lock falling off, and the stock worm-eaten.

---

1 *fear and trembling* Cf. Philippians 2.12: "Wherefore, my beloved, as ye have always obeyed, not as in my presence only, but now much more in my absence, work out your own salvation with fear and trembling."
2 *Hollands* Dutch gin.

He now suspected that the grave roysters[1] of the mountain had put a trick upon him, and having dosed him with liquor, had robbed him of his gun. Wolf, too, had disappeared, but he might have strayed away after a squirrel or partridge. He whistled after him, shouted his name, but all in vain; the echoes repeated his whistle and shout, but no dog was to be seen.

He determined to revisit the scene of the last evening's gambol,[2] and if he met with any of the party, to demand his dog and gun. As he arose to walk he found himself stiff in the joints, and wanting in his usual activity.[3] "These mountain beds do not agree with me," thought Rip, "and if this frolic should lay me up with a fit of the rheumatism, I shall have a blessed time with Dame Van Winkle." With some difficulty he got down into the glen: he found the gully up which he and his companion had ascended the preceding evening, but to his astonishment a mountain stream was now foaming down it, leaping from rock to rock, and filling the glen with babbling murmurs. He, however, made shift to scramble up its sides, working his toilsome way through thickets of birch, sassafras, and witch hazel, and sometimes tripped up or entangled by the wild grape vines that twisted their coils and tendrils from tree to tree, and spread a kind of network in his path.

At length he reached to where the ravine had opened through the cliffs, to the amphitheatre; but no traces of such opening remained. The rocks presented a high impenetrable wall, over which the torrent came tumbling in a sheet of feathery foam, and fell into a broad deep basin, black from the shadows of the surrounding forest. Here, then, poor Rip was brought to a stand. He again called and whistled after his dog; he was only answered by the cawing of a flock of idle crows, sporting high in air about a dry tree that overhung a sunny precipice; and who, secure in their elevation, seemed to look down and scoff at the poor man's perplexities. What was to be done? the morning was passing away, and Rip felt famished for his breakfast. He grieved to give up his dog and gun; he dreaded to meet his wife; but it would not do to starve among the mountains. He shook his head, shouldered the rusty firelock, and, with a heart full of trouble and anxiety, turned his steps homeward.

---

1 *roysters* Revelers.
2 *gambol* Festivity; frolic.
3 *wanting in his usual activity* I.e., lacking his usual energy.

As he approached the village, he met a number of people, but none that he knew, which somewhat surprised him, for he had thought himself acquainted with everyone in the country round. Their dress, too, was of a different fashion from that to which he was accustomed. They all stared at him with equal marks of surprise, and whenever they cast eyes upon him, invariably stroked their chins. The constant recurrence of this gesture induced Rip, involuntarily, to do the same, when, to his astonishment, he found his beard had grown a foot long!

He had now entered the skirts of the village. A troop of strange children ran at his heels, hooting after him, and pointing at his gray beard. The dogs, too, not one of which he recognized for his old acquaintances, barked at him as he passed. The very village seemed altered: it was larger and more populous. There were rows of houses which he had never seen before, and those which had been his familiar haunts had disappeared. Strange names were over the doors—strange faces at the windows—everything was strange. His mind now began to misgive him, that both he and the world around him were bewitched. Surely this was his native village, which he had left but the day before. There stood the Kaatskill mountains—there ran the silver Hudson at a distance—there was every hill and dale precisely as it had always been—Rip was sorely perplexed. "That flagon last night," thought he, "has addled my poor head sadly!"

It was with some difficulty he found the way to his own house, which he approached with silent awe, expecting every moment to hear the shrill voice of Dame Van Winkle. He found the house gone to decay—the roof fallen in, the windows shattered, and the doors off the hinges. A half-starved dog, that looked like Wolf, was skulking about it. Rip called him by name, but the cur snarled, showed his teeth, and passed on. This was an unkind cut indeed. "My very dog," sighed poor Rip, "has forgotten me!"

He entered the house, which, to tell the truth, Dame Van Winkle had always kept in neat order. It was empty, forlorn, and apparently abandoned. This desolateness overcame all his connubial fears—he called loudly for his wife and children—the lonely chambers rung for a moment with his voice, and then all again was silence.

He now hurried forth, and hastened to his old resort, the little village inn—but it too was gone. A large rickety wooden building stood in its place, with great gaping windows, some of them broken, and mended with old hats and petticoats, and over the door was painted, "The Union Hotel, by Jonathan Doolittle." Instead of the great tree that used to shelter the quiet little Dutch inn of yore, there now was reared a tall naked pole, with something on top that looked like a red night cap,[1] and from it was fluttering a flag, on which was a singular assemblage of stars and stripes—all this was strange and incomprehensible. He recognized on the sign, however, the ruby face of King George, under which he had smoked so many a peaceful pipe, but even this was singularly metamorphosed. The red coat was changed for one of blue and buff,[2] a sword was stuck in the hand instead of a sceptre, the head was decorated with a cocked hat,[3] and underneath was painted in large characters, General Washington.

There was, as usual, a crowd of folk about the door, but none that Rip recollected. The very character of the people seemed changed. There was a busy, bustling, disputatious tone about it, instead of the accustomed phlegm and drowsy tranquillity. He looked in vain for the sage Nicholas Vedder, with his broad face, double chin, and fair long pipe, uttering clouds of tobacco smoke instead of idle speeches; or Van Bummel, the schoolmaster, doling forth the contents of an ancient newspaper. In place of these, a lean, bilious-looking fellow, with his pockets full of handbills, was haranguing vehemently about rights of citizens—election—members of congress—liberty— Bunker's hill—heroes of seventy-six[4]—and other words, that were a perfect Babylonish jargon[5] to the bewildered Van Winkle.

The appearance of Rip, with his long, grizzled beard, his rusty fowling piece, his uncouth dress, and the army of women and children had gathered at his heels, soon attracted the attention of the tavern politicians. They crowded around him, eyeing him from

---

1   *tall naked pole … red night cap* The pole and the red cap were both widespread symbols of liberty, especially after their use in the French Revolution; similar loose-fitting caps had been worn in ancient Rome by people emancipated from slavery.

2   *blue and buff* Colors worn by American Revolutionary soldiers.

3   *cocked hat* Style of hat worn in the late eighteenth century (especially as part of military uniforms), with one side of the brim folded up or "cocked."

4   *Bunker's hill* First major battle of the Revolutionary War; *heroes of seventy-six* The Declaration of Independence was drafted in 1776.

5   *Babylonish jargon* Incomprehensible gibberish, referring to the biblical story of the Tower of Babel (Genesis 11.1–9), which relates how it came to be that humans speak different languages and cannot understand one another; technically, the more correct term would be "Babelish."

head to foot, with great curiosity. The orator bustled up to him, and drawing him partly aside, inquired "which side he voted?" Rip stared in vacant stupidity. Another short but busy little fellow pulled him by the arm, and raising on tiptoe, inquired in his ear, "whether he was Federal or Democrat."[1] Rip was equally at a loss to comprehend the question, when a knowing, self-important old gentleman, in a sharp cocked hat, made his way through the crowd, putting them to the right and left with his elbows as he passed, and planting himself before Van Winkle, with one arm akimbo, the other resting on his cane, his keen eyes and sharp hat penetrating, as it were, into his very soul, demanded, in an austere tone, "what brought him to the election with a gun on his shoulder, and a mob at his heels, and whether he meant to breed a riot in the village?" "Alas! gentlemen," cried Rip, somewhat dismayed, "I am a poor quiet man, a native of the place, and a loyal subject of the King, God bless him!"

Here a general shout burst from the bystanders—"A tory![2] a tory! a spy! a refugee! hustle him! away with him!" It was with great difficulty that the self-important man in the cocked hat restored order; and having assumed a tenfold austerity of brow, demanded again of the unknown culprit, what he came there for, and whom he was seeking. The poor man humbly assured them that he meant no harm, but merely came there in search of some of his neighbours, who used to keep about the tavern.

"Well—who are they?—name them."

Rip bethought himself a moment, and inquired, "where's Nicholas Vedder?"

There was a silence for a little while, when an old man replied, in a thin piping voice, "Nicholas Vedder? why he is dead and gone these eighteen years! There was a wooden tombstone in the churchyard that used to tell all about him, but that's rotted and gone too."

"Where's Brom Dutcher?"

---

1   *Federal or Democrat*   Opposing political parties that arose in the 1790s, led respectively by Alexander Hamilton (1755–1804) and Thomas Jefferson (1743–1826); the policies of the Federalists emphasized a strong central government and favored stronger ties to Britain in foreign affairs, while Jefferson's Democratic-Republicans placed more emphasis on states' rights, defended the values of an agrarian society in opposition to the perceived elitism of the Federalists, and believed in the capability of common people to participate fully in democracy.
2   *tory*   Royalist.

"Oh he went off to the army in the beginning of the war; some say he was killed at the battle of Stoney Point—others say he was drowned in a squall, at the foot of Antony's Nose.[1] I don't know—he never came back again."

"Where's Van Bummel, the schoolmaster?"

"He went off to the wars too, was a great militia general, and is now in Congress."

Rip's heart died away, at hearing of these sad changes in his home and friends, and finding himself thus alone in the world. Every answer puzzled him, too, by treating of such enormous lapses of time, and of matters which he could not understand: war—congress—Stoney Point—he had no courage to ask after any more friends, but cried out in despair, "does nobody here know Rip Van Winkle?"

"Oh, Rip Van Winkle!" exclaimed two or three, "Oh, to be sure! that's Rip Van Winkle yonder, leaning against the tree."

Rip looked, and beheld a precise counterpart of himself as he went up the mountain: apparently as lazy, and certainly as ragged. The poor fellow was now completely confounded. He doubted his own identity, and whether he was himself or another man. In the midst of his bewilderment, the man in the cocked hat demanded who he was, and what was his name?

"God knows," exclaimed he, at his wit's end; "I'm not myself—I'm somebody else—that's me yonder—no—that's somebody else, got into my shoes—I was myself last night, but I fell asleep on the mountain, and they've changed my gun, and everything's changed, and I'm changed, and I can't tell what's my name, or who I am!"

The bystanders began now to look at each other, nod, wink significantly, and tap their fingers against their foreheads. There was a whisper, also, about securing the gun, and keeping the old fellow from doing mischief; at the very suggestion of which, the self-important man in the cocked hat retired with some precipitation. At this critical moment a fresh likely[2] woman pressed through the throng to get a peep at the graybearded man. She had a chubby child in her arms, which, frightened at his looks, began to cry. "Hush, Rip," cried

---

1 *Stoney Point* British fortress that was captured by the Continental Army in 1779; *Antony's Nose* Small mountain along the Hudson River, which is also mentioned in Irving's *History of New York*.

2 *likely* Pretty (later revised editions have "comely" here).

she, "hush, you little fool, the old man won't hurt you." The name of the child, the air of the mother, the tone of her voice, all awakened a train of recollections in his mind.

"What is your name, my good woman?" asked he.

"Judith Gardenier."

"And your father's name?"

"Ah, poor man, his name was Rip Van Winkle; it's twenty years since he went away from home with his gun, and never has been heard of since—his dog came home without him; but whether he shot himself, or was carried away by the Indians, nobody can tell. I was then but a little girl."

Rip had but one question more to ask; but he put it with a faltering voice:

"Where's your mother?"

Oh, she too had died but a short time since; she broke a blood vessel in a fit of passion at a New England pedlar.

There was a drop of comfort, at least, in this intelligence. The honest man could contain himself no longer. He caught his daughter and her child in his arms. "I am your father!" cried he—"Young Rip Van Winkle once—old Rip Van Winkle now! Does nobody know poor Rip Van Winkle?"

All stood amazed, until an old woman, tottering out from among the crowd, put her hand to her brow, and peering under it in his face for a moment, exclaimed, "Sure enough! it is Rip Van Winkle—it is himself. Welcome home again, old neighbour—why, where have you been these twenty long years?"

Rip's story was soon told, for the whole twenty years had been to him but as one night. The neighbours stared when they heard it; some were seen to wink at each other, and put their tongues in their cheeks; and the self-important man in the cocked hat, who, when the alarm was over, had returned to the field, screwed down the corners of his mouth, and shook his head—upon which there was a general shaking of the head throughout the assemblage.

It was determined, however, to take the opinion of old Peter Vanderdonk, who was seen slowly advancing up the road. He was a descendant of the historian of that name,[1] who wrote one of the earliest

---

1 *historian of that name*   Adriaen van der Donk, who wrote *Description of New Netherland* (1655).

accounts of the province. Peter was the most ancient inhabitant of the village, and well versed in all the wonderful events and traditions of the neighbourhood. He recollected Rip at once, and corroborated his story in the most satisfactory manner. He assured the company that it was a fact, handed down from his ancestor the historian, that the Kaatskill mountains had always been haunted by strange beings. That it was affirmed that the great Hendrick Hudson, the first discoverer of the river and country, kept a kind of vigil there every twenty years, with his crew of the Half-moon,[1] being permitted in this way to revisit the scenes of his enterprise, and keep a guardian eye upon the river, and the great city called by his name. That his father had once seen them in their old Dutch dresses playing at nine pins in a hollow of the mountain; and that he himself had heard, one summer afternoon, the sound of their balls, like long peals of thunder.

To make a long story short, the company broke up, and returned to the more important concerns of the election. Rip's daughter took him home to live with her; she had a snug, well-furnished house, and a stout cheery farmer for a husband, whom Rip recollected for one of the urchins that used to climb upon his back. As to Rip's son and heir, who was the ditto of himself, seen leaning against the tree, he was employed to work on the farm; but evinced an hereditary disposition to attend to anything else but his business.

Rip now resumed his old walks and habits; he soon found many of his former cronies, though all rather the worse for the wear and tear of time; and preferred making friends among the rising generation, with whom he soon grew into great favour.

Having nothing to do at home, and being arrived at that happy age when a man can do nothing with impunity, he took his place once more on the bench, at the inn door, and was reverenced as one of the patriarchs of the village, and a chronicle of the old times "before the war." It was some time before he could get into the regular track of gossip, or could be made to comprehend the strange events that had taken place during his torpor. How that there had been a revolutionary war—that the country had thrown off the yoke of old England—and that, instead of being a subject of his Majesty George the Third,

---

1   *crew of the Half-moon* Referring to Hudson's ship, the *Halve Maen*; following a mutiny in 1611, Hudson and seven other crew members disappeared into Hudson Bay, their fates remaining unknown.

he was now a free citizen of the United States. Rip, in fact, was no politician; the change of states and empires made but little impression on him. But there was one species of despotism under which he had long groaned, and that was—petticoat government. Happily, that was at an end; he had got his neck out of the yoke of matrimony, and could go in and out whenever he pleased, without dreading the tyranny of Dame Van Winkle. Whenever her name was mentioned, however, he shook his head, shrugged his shoulders, and cast up his eyes; which might pass either for an expression of resignation to his fate, or joy at his deliverance.

He used to tell his story to every stranger that arrived at Mr. Doolittle's hotel. He was observed, at first, to vary on some points every time he told it, which was doubtless owing to his having so recently awakened. It at last settled down precisely to the tale I have related, and not a man, woman, or child in the neighbourhood, but knew it by heart. Some always pretended to doubt the reality of it, and insisted that Rip had been out of his head, and that this was one point on which he always remained flighty. The old Dutch inhabitants, however, almost universally gave it full credit. Even to this day they never hear a thunderstorm of a summer afternoon about the Kaatskill, but they say Hendrick Hudson and his crew are at their game of nine pins; and it is a common wish of all henpecked husbands in the neighbourhood, when life hangs heavy on their hands, that they might have a quieting draught out of Rip Van Winkle's flagon.

NOTE

The foregoing tale, one would suspect, had been suggested to Mr. Knickerbocker by a little German superstition about Charles V.[1] and the Kypphauser mountain; the subjoined note, however, which he

---

1 *Charles V.* Holy Roman Emperor from 1519 to 1556. In later editions, Irving changed this to "the Emperor Frederick der Rothbart," another Holy Roman Emperor who reigned from 1152 to 1190. According to legend, der Rothbart, also known as Frederick Barbarossa ("redbeard"), did not die but rather fell asleep in the Kyffhäuser mountains in Germany, and will one day reawaken and return Germany to its past greatness. In reality, Irving's source for "Rip Van Winkle" is likely the German folktale "Peter Klaus," which was written down by Johann Karl Christoph Nachtigal in 1800.

had appended to the tale, shows that it is an absolute fact, narrated with his usual fidelity:

"The story of Rip Van Winkle may seem incredible to many, but nevertheless I give it my full belief, for I know the vicinity of our old Dutch settlements to have been very subject to marvellous events and appearances. Indeed, I have heard many stranger stories than this, in the villages along the Hudson; all of which were too well authenticated to admit of a doubt. I have even talked with Rip Van Winkle myself, who, when last I saw him, was a very venerable old man, and so perfectly rational and consistent on every other point, that I think no conscientious person could refuse to take this into the bargain; nay, I have seen a certificate on the subject taken before a country justice, and signed with a cross, in the justice's own hand writing. The story, therefore, is beyond the possibility of doubt.
D.K."

—1819

English Writers on America

"Methinks I see in my mind a noble and puissant nation, rousing herself, like a strong man after sleep, and shaking her invincible locks: methinks I see her as an eagle, mewing her mighty youth, and kindling her endazzled eyes at the full mid-day beam."

MILTON ON THE LIBERTY OF THE PRESS[1]

It is with feelings of deep regret that I have noticed the literary animosity daily growing up between England and America. Great curiosity has been awakened of late with respect to the United States, and the London press has teemed with volumes of travels through the republic; but they seem intended to diffuse error rather than knowledge; and so successful have they been, that, notwithstanding the constant intercourse between the nations, there is none concerning which the great mass of the British people have less pure information, or more prejudices.

English travellers are the best and the worst in the world. Where no motives of pride or interest intervene, none can equal them for profound and philosophical views of society, or faithful and graphical descriptions of external objects; but when the interests or reputation of their own nation come in collision with those of another, they go to the opposite extreme, and forget their usual probity and candour, in the indulgence of spleen, and an illiberal spirit of ridicule.

Hence, their travels are more honest and accurate, the more remote the country described. I would place implicit confidence in an Englishman's description of the regions beyond the cataracts of the Nile; of unknown islands in the Yellow Sea; of the interior of Africa; or of any other tract which other travellers might be apt to picture out with the illusions of their fancies; but I would cautiously receive his account of his immediate neighbours, and of those nations with which he is in habits of most frequent intercourse. However I might be disposed to trust his probity, I dare not trust his prejudices.

---

1   MILTON ON THE LIBERTY OF THE PRESS   I.e., John Milton's *Areopagitica; A speech of Mr. John Milton for the Liberty of Unlicenc'd Printing, to the Parliament of England* (1644).

But it has been the peculiar lot of our country, to be visited by the worst kind of English travellers. While men of philosophical spirit and cultivated minds have been envoys from England to ransack the poles, to penetrate the deserts, and to study the manners and customs of barbarous nations, with which she can have no permanent intercourse of profit or pleasure; it is left to the broken down tradesman, the scheming adventurer, the wandering mechanic, the Manchester and Birmingham agent, to be her oracles respecting America—to treat of a country in a singular state of moral and physical development; where one of the greatest political experiments in the history of the world is now performing, and which presents the most profound and momentous studies for the statesman and the philosopher.

That such men should give prejudiced accounts of America is not a matter of surprise. The themes it offers for contemplation are too vast and elevated for their capacities. The national character is yet in a state of fermentation: it may have its frothiness and sediment, but its ingredients are sound and wholesome: it has already given proofs of powerful and generous qualities, and the whole promises to settle down into something substantially excellent. But the causes that are operating to strengthen and ennoble it, and its daily indications of admirable properties, are all lost upon these purblind[1] observers, who are only affected by the little asperities incident to its present situation. They are capable of judging only of the surface of things; of those matters which come in contact with their private interests and gratifications. They miss some of the snug conveniences and petty comforts which belong to an old, highly finished, and over-populous state of society, where the ranks of useful labour are crowded, and many make a painful and servile subsistence, by studying the very caprices of appetite and self indulgence. These minor comforts, however, are all-important in the estimation of narrow minds; and they either do not perceive, or will not acknowledge, that they are more than counterbalanced among us, by great and generally diffused blessings.

Or, perhaps, they have been disappointed in some unreasonable expectation of sudden gain. They may have pictured America themselves an El Dorado,[2] where gold and silver abounded, and the natives

---

1   *purblind*   Short sighted.
2   *El Dorado*   Legendary city of wealth and beauty believed to have existed in the Americas.

were lacking in sagacity. Where they were to become strangely and suddenly rich, in some unforeseen but easy manner. The same weakness of mind that indulges absurd expectations, produces petulance in disappointment. They become embittered against the country on finding that there, as everywhere else, a man must sow before he can reap; that he must win wealth by industry and talent; and must compete with the common difficulties of nature, and the shrewdness of an intelligent and enterprising people.

Or perhaps, through mistake, or ill-directed hospitality, or the prompt disposition to cheer and countenance the stranger, prevalent among my countrymen, they may have been treated with unwonted respect in America; and, accustomed all their lives to consider themselves many strata below the surface of society, and brought up in a servile feeling of inferiority, they become arrogant on the common boon of civility; they attribute to the lowliness of others their own elevation; and underrate a society where there are no artificial distinctions, and where, by any chance, such individuals as themselves can rise to consequence.

One would suppose, however, that information coming from such sources, on a subject where the truth is so desirable, would be received with caution by the censors of the press. That the motives of these men, their veracity, their opportunities of inquiry and observation, and their capacities for judging correctly, would be rigorously scrutinized, before their evidence was admitted, in such sweeping extent, against a kindred nation. The very reverse, however, is the case, and it furnishes a striking instance of human inconsistency. Nothing can surpass the vigilance with which English critics will test the credibility of the traveller who publishes an account of some distant, and comparatively unimportant, country. How warily will they compare the measurements of a pyramid, or the descriptions of a ruin, and how sternly will they censure any discrepancy in these contributions of merely curious knowledge; while they will receive, with eagerness and unhesitating faith, the gross misrepresentations of coarse and obscure writers, concerning a country with which their own is placed in the most important and delicate relations. Nay, what is worse, they will make these apocryphal volumes textbooks, on which to enlarge, with a zeal and an ability worthy of a more generous cause.

I shall not, however, dwell on this irksome and hackneyed topic; nor should I have adverted to it, but for the undue interest apparently taken in it by my countrymen, and certain injurious effects which I apprehended it might produce upon the national feeling. We attach too much consequence to these attacks. They cannot do us any essential injury. The tissue of misrepresentations attempted to be woven round us, are like cobwebs wove round the limbs of an infant giant. Our country continually outgrows them. One falsehood after another falls off of itself. We have but to live on, and every day we live a whole volume of refutation. All the writers of England, united, cannot conceal our rapidly growing importance and matchless prosperity. They cannot conceal that these are owing not merely to physical and local, but to moral causes. To the political liberty, the general diffusion of knowledge, the prevalence of sound moral and religious principles, that give force and sustained energy to the character of a people; and which, in fact, have been acknowledged and wonderful supporters of their own national power and glory.

But why are we so exquisitely alive to the aspersions of England? Why do we suffer ourselves to be so affected by the contumely she has endeavoured to cast upon us? It is not in the opinion of England alone that honour lives, and reputation has its being. The world at large is the arbiter of a nation's fame: with its thousand eyes it witnesses a nation's deeds, and from their collective testimony is national glory or disgrace established.

For ourselves, therefore, it is comparatively of but little importance whether England do us justice or not: it is, perhaps, of far more importance to herself. She is instilling anger and resentment into the bosom of a youthful nation, to grow with its growth, and strengthen with its strength. If in America, as some of her writers are labouring to convince her, she is hereafter to find an invidious rival, and a gigantic foe, she may thank those very writers for having provoked that rivalship, and irritated that hostility. Everyone knows the all-pervading influence of literature at the present day, and how completely the opinions and passions of mankind are under its control. The mere contests of the sword are temporary; their wounds are but in the flesh, and it is the pride of the generous to forgive and forget them; but the slanders of the pen pierce to the heart; they rankle most sorely and permanently in the noblest spirits; they dwell ever present in the mind, and make it morbidly sensitive to the most trifling collision. It is not so much any one overt act that produces hostilities between two nations; there exists, most commonly, a previous jealousy and ill will, a predisposition to take offence. Trace these to their cause, and how often will they be found to originate in the mischievous effusions of writers, who, secure in their closets, and for ignominious bread, concoct and circulate the venom that is to inflame the generous and the brave.

I am not laying too much stress upon this point; for it applies most emphatically to our particular case. Over no nation does the press hold a more absolute control than over the people of America; for the universal education of the poorest classes makes every individual a reader. There is nothing published in England on the subject of our country, that does not circulate through every part of it. There is not a calumny[1] dropt from an English pen, nor an unworthy sarcasm uttered by an English statesman, that does not go to blight good will, and add to the mass of latent resentment. Possessing, then, as England does, the fountainhead from whence the literature of the language flows, how completely is it in her power, and how truly is it her duty, to make it the medium of amiable and magnanimous feeling—a stream where the two nations might meet together, and drink in peace and kindness. Should she, however, persist in turning it to waters of bitterness, the time may come when she may repent her folly. The present friendship of America may be of but little moment to her; but the future destinies of that country do not admit of a doubt: over those of England there lower some shadows of uncertainty. Should, then, a day of gloom arrive; should those reverses overtake her, from which the proudest empires have not been exempt, she may look back with regret at her infatuation, in repulsing from her side a nation she might have grappled to her bosom, and thus destroying her only chance for real friendship beyond the boundaries of her own dominions.

There is a general impression in England, that the people of the United States are inimical to the parent country. It is one of the errors that has been diligently propagated by designing writers. There is, doubtless, considerable political hostility, and a general soreness at the illiberality of the English press; but, collectively speaking, the prepossessions of the people are strongly in favour of England. Indeed, at one time they amounted, in many parts of the union, to a degree of

---

1   *calumny*   Slanderous claim.

bigotry that was absurd. The bare name of Englishman was a passport to the confidence and hospitality of every family, and too often gave a transient currency to the worthless and the ungrateful. Throughout the country there was something of enthusiasm connected with the idea of England. We looked to it with a hallowed feeling of tenderness and veneration, as the land of our forefathers—the august repository of the monuments and antiquities of our race—the birthplace and mausoleum of the sages and heroes of our paternal history. After our own country, there was none in whose glory we more delighted—none whose good opinion we were more anxious of possessing—none toward whom our hearts yearned with such throbbings of warm consanguinity. Even during the late war, whenever there was the least opportunity for kind feelings to spring forth, it was the delight of the generous spirits of the country to show that, in the midst of hostilities, they still kept alive the sparks of future friendship.

Is all this to be at an end? Is this golden band of kindred sympathies, so rare between nations, to be broken forever? Perhaps it is for the best—it may dispel an illusion which might have kept us in mental vassalage, interfered occasionally with our true interests, and prevented the growth of proper national pride. But it is hard to give up the kindred tie! and there are feelings dearer than interest—closer to the heart than pride—that will still make us cast back a look of regret, as we wander farther and farther from the paternal roof, and lament the waywardness of the parent, that would not permit the affections of the child.

But however short-sighted and injudicious may be the conduct of England in this system of aspersion, recrimination on our part would be equally ill-judged. I speak not of a prompt and spirited vindication of our country, or the keenest castigation of her slanderers—but I allude to a disposition to retaliate in kind, to retort sarcasm and inspire prejudice, which seems to be spreading widely among our writers. Let us guard particularly against such a temper, for it would double the injury, instead of redressing it. Nothing is so easy and inviting as the retort of abuse and sarcasm; but it is a paltry and unprofitable contest. It is the alternative of a morbid mind, fretted into petulance, rather than warmed into indignation. If England is willing to permit the mean jealousies of trade, or the rancorous animosities of politics, to deprave the integrity of her press, and poison the fountain of public opinion, let us not follow her example. She may deem it her interest to diffuse error, and engender antipathy, for the purpose of checking emigration; we have no purpose of the kind to serve. Neither can we have any spirit of national jealousy to gratify, for as yet, in all our rivalships with England, we are the rising and the gaining party. There can be no end to answer, therefore, but the gratification of resentment—a mere spirit of retaliation. But even that is impotent. Our retorts are never republished in England; and fall short, therefore, of their aim; but they foster a querulous and peevish temper among our writers; they sour the sweet flow of our early literature, and sow thorns and brambles among its blossoms; but what is still worse, they circulate over our own country, and, as far as they have effect, produce virulent national prejudices. This last is the evil most especially to be deprecated. Governed, as we are, entirely by public opinion, the utmost care should be taken to preserve the purity of the public mind. Knowledge is power, and truth is knowledge; whoever, therefore, knowingly propagates a prejudice, wilfully saps the foundation of his country's strength.

Republicans,[1] above all other men, should be characterized by candour and clearness of thinking. They are, individually, portions of the sovereign mind and sovereign will, and should be enabled to come to all questions of national concern with calm, unbiased judgments. From the peculiar nature of our relations with England, also, we must have more frequent questions of a difficult and delicate character arising between us than with any other nation; questions that affect the most acute and excitable feelings: and as these must ultimately be determined by popular sentiment, we cannot be too anxiously attentive to purify it from all latent passion or prepossession.

Opening too, as we do, an asylum for all nations of the earth, we should receive them all with impartiality. It should be our pride to exhibit an example of one nation at least, destitute of national antipathies, and exercising, not merely the overt acts of hospitality, but those more rare and noble courtesies which spring from liberality of opinion.

Indeed, what have we to do with national prejudices? They are the inveterate diseases of old countries, that have crept into their

---

1 *Republicans* I.e., members of a republic.

habits of thinking in rude and ignorant ages, when nations knew but little of each other, and looked beyond their own boundaries with distrust and hostility. But we have sprung into national existence in an enlightened and philosophic age, when the different parts of the habitable world, and the various branches of the human family, have been indefatigably studied and made known to each other; and we discredit the advantages of our birth, if we do not shake off the national prejudices, as we would the local superstitions, of the old world.

But above all, let us not be influenced by any angry feelings, so far as to shut our eyes to the perception of what is really excellent and amiable in the English character. We are a young people, and an imitative one, and will form ourselves upon the older nations of Europe. There is no country so worthy of our study as England. The spirit of her constitution is most analogous to ours. The manners of her people—their intellectual activity—their freedom of opinion—their habits of thinking on all subjects that concern the dearest interests and most sacred charities of private life, are all most congenial to the American character; and, in fact, are most worthy in themselves: for it is in the moral feeling of the people that the deep foundations of British prosperity are laid; and however the superstructure may be time-worn, or overrun by abuses, there must be something solid in its basis, and admirable in its materials, to uphold it so long unshaken by the tempests of the world.

It should be the endeavour of our writers, therefore, discarding all feelings of irritation, and disdaining to be affected by the illiberality of British authors, to speak of the nation dispassionately, and with determined candour. While they rebuke the indiscriminating bigotry with which some of their countrymen admire and imitate everything English, merely because it is English, they should point out what is really worthy of approbation. We may thus place England before us as a perpetual volume of reference, wherein the sound deductions of ages of experience are recorded; and while we avoid the errors and absurdities which may have crept into the page, we may draw from thence golden maxims of practical wisdom, wherewith to strengthen and embellish our national character.

—1819

Traits of Indian Character

The 1820 English edition of Irving's *Sketch Book* includes several pieces that did not appear in the American edition of 1819; "Traits of Indian Character" is one of these. The essay was not, however, entirely new. The version that appears on left-hand pages below was published in the February 1814 issue of *The Analectic Magazine*, a Philadelphia monthly that Irving edited in 1813–14. Original articles were the exception rather than the rule in *The Analectic*, which advertised itself as presenting "selections from foreign reviews and magazines of such articles as are most valuable, curious, or entertaining." As can be seen in this facing-page presentation, Irving revised the piece substantially for publication in the English edition of his *Sketch Book*. (Another point of comparison in Irving's writings on Native Americans may be found in Chapter 5 of *A History of New York, from the Beginning of the World to the End of the Dutch Dynasty, by Dietrich Knickerbocker*; see pages 13–25 above.)

In the present times, when popular feeling is gradually becoming hardened by war, and selfish by the frequent jeopardy of life or property, it is certainly an inauspicious moment to speak in behalf of a race of beings, whose very existence has been pronounced detrimental to public security. But it is good at all times to raise the voice of truth, however feeble; to endeavour, if possible, to mitigate the fury of passion and prejudice, and to turn aside the bloody hand of violence. Little interest, however, can probably be awakened at present, in favour of the misguided tribes of Indians that have been drawn into the present war.[1] The rights of the savage have seldom been deeply appreciated by the white man—in peace he is the dupe of mercenary rapacity; in war he is regarded as a ferocious animal, whose death is a question of mere precaution and convenience. Man is cruelly wasteful of life when his own safety is endangered and he is sheltered by impunity—and little mercy is to be expected from him who feels the sting of the reptile, and is conscious of the power to destroy.

It has been the lot of the unfortunate aborigines of this country, to be doubly wronged by the white men—first, driven from their native soil by the sword of the invader, and then darkly slandered by the pen of the historian. The former has treated them like beasts of the forest; the latter has written volumes to justify him in his outrages. The former found it easier to exterminate than to civilize; the latter to abuse than to discriminate. The hideous appellations of savage and pagan, were sufficient to sanction the deadly hostilities of both; and the poor wanderers of the forest were persecuted and dishonoured, not because they were guilty, but because they were ignorant.

---

1   *the present war*   Irving refers to the War of 1812—which in fact lasted until 1815—in which many Native American tribes allied themselves with the British against the United States.

"I appeal to any white man if ever he entered Logan's cabin hungry, and he gave him not to eat; if ever he came cold and naked, and he clothed him not."

SPEECH OF AN INDIAN CHIEF[1]

There is something in the character and habits of the North American savage, taken in connexion with the scenery over which he is accustomed to range, its vast lakes, boundless forests, majestic rivers and trackless plains, that is, to my mind, wonderfully striking and sublime. He is formed for the wilderness, as the Arab is for the desert. His nature is stern, simple and enduring; fitted to grapple with difficulties, and to support privations. There seems but little soil in his heart for the growth of the kindly virtues; and yet, if we would but take the trouble to penetrate through that proud stoicism and habitual taciturnity, which lock up his character from casual observation, we should find him linked to his fellow man of civilized life by more of those sympathies and affections than are usually ascribed to him.

It has been the lot of the unfortunate aborigines of America, in the early periods of colonization, to be doubly wronged by the white men. They have been dispossessed of their hereditary possessions by mercenary and frequently wanton warfare; and their characters have been traduced by bigoted and interested writers. The colonist has often treated them like beasts of the forest; and the author has endeavoured to justify him in his outrages. The former found it easier to exterminate than to civilize; the latter to vilify than to discriminate. The appellations of savage and pagan were deemed sufficient to sanction the hostilities of both; and thus the poor wanderers of the

---

1   *SPEECH OF AN INDIAN CHIEF*   Words from a speech historically attributed to Logan, a Cayuga leader in the Iroquois Confederacy, who fought with the Shawnee and Mingo in the conflict known as Dunmore's War following the murder of his family; the speech, popularly known as "Logan's Lament," was reprinted in newspapers in 1774 as well as in Thomas Jefferson's *Notes on the State of Virginia* (1787).

The same prejudices seem to exist, in common circulation, at the present day. We form our opinions of the Indian character from the miserable hordes that infest our frontiers. These, however, are degenerate beings, enfeebled by the vices of society, without being benefited by its arts of living. The independence of thought and action that formed the main pillar of their character has been completely prostrated, and the whole moral fabric lies in ruins. Their spirits are debased by conscious inferiority, and their native courage completely daunted by the superior knowledge and power of their enlightened neighbours. Society has advanced upon them like a many-headed monster, breathing every variety of misery. Before it went forth pestilence, famine, and the sword; and in its train came the slow, but exterminating curse of trade. What the former did not sweep away, the latter has gradually blighted. It has increased their wants, without increasing the means of gratification. It has enervated their strength, multiplied their diseases, blasted the powers of their minds, and superinduced on their original barbarity the low vices of civilization. Poverty, repining and hopeless poverty—a canker of the mind unknown to sylvan[1] life—corrodes their very hearts. They loiter like vagrants through the settlements, among spacious habitations replete with artificial comforts, which only render them sensible of the comparative wretchedness of their own condition. Luxury spreads its ample board before their eyes, but they are expelled from the banquet. The forest which once furnished them with ample means of subsistence has been levelled to the ground—waving fields of grain have sprung up in its place; but they have no participation in

---

1   *sylvan* Woodland.

forest were persecuted and defamed, not because they were guilty, but because they were ignorant.

The rights of the savage have seldom been properly appreciated or respected by the white man. In peace he has too often been the dupe of artful traffic; in war he has been regarded as a ferocious animal, whose life or death was a question of mere precaution and convenience. Man is cruelly wasteful of life when his own safety is endangered, and he is sheltered by impunity; and little mercy is to be expected from him when he feels the sting of the reptile and is conscious of the power to destroy.

The same prejudices which were indulged thus early, exist in common circulation at the present day. Certain learned societies have, it is true, with laudable diligence, endeavoured to investigate and record the real characters and manners of the Indian tribes; the American government too, has wisely and humanely exerted itself to inculcate a friendly and forbearing spirit towards them, and to protect them from fraud and injustice.[1] The current opinion of the Indian character, however, is too apt to be formed from the miserable hordes which infest the frontiers, and hang on the skirts of the settlements. These are too commonly composed of degenerate beings, corrupted and enfeebled by the vices of society, without being benefited by its civilization. That proud independence, which formed the main pillar of savage virtue, has been shaken down, and the whole moral fabric lies in ruins. Their spirits are humiliated and debased by a sense of inferiority, and their native courage cowed and daunted by the superior knowledge and power of their enlightened neighbours. Society has advanced upon them like one of those withering airs that will sometimes breathe desolation over a whole region of fertility. It has enervated their strength, multiplied their diseases, and superinduced upon their original barbarity the low vices of artificial life. It has given them a thousand superfluous wants, whilst it has diminished their means of

---

1 [Irving's note]   The American government has been indefatigable in its exertions to ameliorate the situation of the Indians, and to introduce among them the arts of civilization, and civil and religious knowledge. To protect them from the frauds of the white traders, no purchase of land from them by individuals is permitted; nor is any person allowed to receive lands from them as a present, without the express sanction of government. These precautions are strictly enforced.

the harvest; plenty reveals around them, but they are starving amidst its stores; the whole wilderness blossoms like a garden, but they feel like the reptiles that infest it.

How different was their case while yet the undisputed lords of the soil. Their wants were few, and the means of gratifying them within their reach. They saw everyone around them sharing the same lot, enduring the same hardships, living in the same cabins, feeding on the same aliments,[1] arrayed in the same rude garments. No roof then rose, but what was open to the houseless stranger; no smoke curled among the trees, but he was welcomed to sit down by its fire, and join the hunter in his repast. "For," says an old historian of New England, "their life is so void of care, and they are so loving also, that they make use of those things they enjoy as common goods, and are therein so compassionate that rather than one should starve through want, they would starve all: thus do they pass their time merrily, not regarding our pomp, but are better content with their own, which some men esteem so meanly of."[2] Such were the Indians while in the pride and energy of primitive simplicity: they resemble those wild plants that thrive best in the shades of the forest, but which shrink from the hand of cultivation, and perish beneath the influence of the sun.

---

1   *aliments*   Foods.
2   *For ... meanly of*   See Thomas Morton's *New English Canaan* (1637), Book One, Chapter Twenty.

mere existence. It has driven before it the animals of the chase, who fly from the sound of the axe and the smoke of the settlement, and seek refuge in the depths of remoter forests and yet untrodden wilds. Thus do we too often find the Indians on our frontiers to be mere wrecks and remnants of once powerful tribes, who have lingered in the vicinity of the settlements, and sunk into precarious and vagabond existence. Poverty, repining and hopeless poverty, a canker of the mind unknown in savage life, corrodes their spirits and blights every free and noble quality of their natures. They become drunken, indolent, feeble, thievish and pusillanimous. They loiter like vagrants about the settlements, among spacious dwellings, replete with elaborate comforts, which only render them sensible of the comparative wretchedness of their own condition. Luxury spreads its ample board before their eyes, but they are excluded from the banquet. Plenty revels over the fields, but they are starving in the midst of its abundance; the whole wilderness has blossomed into a garden; but they feel as reptiles that infest it.

How different was their state while yet the undisputed lords of the soil. Their wants were few, and the means of gratification within their reach. They saw everyone round them sharing the same lot, enduring the same hardships, feeding on the same aliments, arrayed in the same rude garments. No roof then rose, but was open to the homeless stranger; no smoke curled among the trees, but he was welcome to sit down by its fire and join the hunter in his repast. "For," says an old historian of New England, "their life is so void of care, and they are so loving also, that they make use of those things they enjoy as common goods, and are therein so compassionate, that rather than one should starve through want, they would starve all; thus do they pass their time merrily, not regarding our pomp, but are better content with their own, which some men esteem so meanly of." Such were the Indians whilst in the pride and energy of their primitive natures; they resemble those wild plants which thrive best in the shades of the forest, but shrink from the hand of cultivation, and perish beneath the influence of the sun.

In the general mode of estimating the savage character, we may perceive a vast degree of vulgar prejudice, and passionate exaggeration, without any of the temperate discussion of true philosophy. No allowance is made for the difference of circumstances, and the operations of principles under which they have been educated. Virtue and vice, though radically the same, yet differ widely in their influence on human conduct, according to the habits and maxims of the society in which the individual is reared. No being acts more rigidly from rule than the Indian. His whole conduct is regulated according to some general maxims early implanted in his mind. The moral laws that govern him, to be sure, are but few, but then he conforms to them all. The white man abounds in laws of religion, morals, and manners; but how many does he violate?

A common cause of accusation against the Indians is the faithlessness of their friendships, and their sudden provocations to hostility. But we do not make allowance for their peculiar modes of thinking and feeling, and the principles by which they are governed. Besides, the friendship of the whites towards the poor Indians, was ever cold, distrustful, oppressive, and insulting. In the intercourse with our frontiers they are seldom treated with confidence, and are frequently subject to injury and encroachment. The solitary savage feels silently but acutely; his sensibilities are not diffused over so wide a surface as those of the white man, but they run in steadier and deeper channels. His pride, his affections, his superstitions, are all directed towards fewer objects, but the wounds inflicted on them are proportionably severe, and furnish motives of hostility which we cannot sufficiently appreciate. Where a community is also limited in number, and forms, as in an Indian tribe, one great patriarchal family, the injury of the individual is the injury of the whole; and as their body politic is small, the sentiment of vengeance is almost instantaneously diffused. One council fire is sufficient to decide the measure. Eloquence and superstition combine to inflame their minds. The orator awakens all their martial ardour, and they are wrought up to a kind of religious desperation, by the visions of the Prophet and the Dreamer.

In discussing the savage character, writers have been too prone to indulge in vulgar prejudice and passionate exaggeration, instead of the candid temper of true philosophy. They have not sufficiently considered the peculiar circumstances in which the Indians have been placed, and the peculiar principles under which they have been educated. No being acts more rigidly from rule than the Indian. His whole conduct is regulated according to some general maxims early implanted in his mind. The moral laws that govern him are, to be sure, but few; but then he conforms to them all; the white man abounds in laws of religion, morals and manners, but how many does he violate!

A frequent ground of accusation against the Indians is their disregard of treaties, and the treachery and wantonness with which, in time of apparent peace, they will suddenly fly to hostilities. The intercourse of the white men with the Indians, however, is too apt to be cold, distrustful, oppressive, and insulting. They seldom treat them with that confidence and frankness which are indispensable to real friendship; nor is sufficient caution observed not to offend against those feelings of pride or superstition, which often prompt the Indian to hostility quicker than mere considerations of interest. The solitary savage feels silently, but acutely. His sensibilities are not diffused over so wide a surface as those of the white man; but they run in steadier and deeper channels. His pride, his affections, his superstitions, are all directed towards fewer objects; but the wounds inflicted on them are proportionably severe, and furnish motives of hostility which we cannot sufficiently appreciate. Where a community is also limited in number, and forms one great patriarchal family, as in an Indian tribe, the injury of an individual is the injury of the whole; and the sentiment of vengeance is almost instantaneously diffused. One council fire is sufficient for the discussion and arrangement of a plan of hostilities. Here all the fighting men and sages assemble. Eloquence and superstition combine to inflame the minds of the warriors. The orator awakens their martial ardour, and they are wrought up to a kind of religious desperation, by the visions of the prophet and the dreamer.

An instance of one of these sudden exasperations, arising from a motive peculiar to the Indian character, is extant in an old record of the early settlement of Massachusetts. The planters of Plymouth had defaced the monuments of the dead at Passonagessit, and had plundered the grave of the sachem's mother of some skins with which it had been piously decorated.[1] Everyone knows the hallowed reverence which the Indians entertain for the sepulchres of their kindred. Even now, tribes that have passed generations exiled from the abodes of their ancestors, when by chance they have been travelling, on some mission, to our seat of government, have been known to turn aside from the highway, for many miles distance, and guided by wonderfully accurate tradition, have sought some tumulus,[2] buried perhaps in woods, where the bones of their tribe were anciently deposited; and there have passed some time in silent lamentation over the ashes of their forefathers. Influenced by this sublime and holy feeling, the sachem whose mother's tomb had been violated, in the moment of indignation, gathered his men together, and addressed them in the following beautifully simple and pathetic[3] harangue—an harangue which has remained unquoted for nearly two hundred years—a pure specimen of Indian eloquence, and an affecting monument of filial piety in a savage.

"When last the glorious light of all the sky was underneath this globe, and birds grew silent, I began to settle, as my custom is, to take repose. Before mine eyes were fast closed, methought I saw a vision, at which my spirit was much troubled, and, trembling at that doleful sight, a spirit cried aloud—behold my son, whom I have cherished; see the breasts that gave thee suck, the hands that lapped thee warm and fed thee oft! Canst thou forget to take revenge of those wild people, who have defaced my monument in a despiteful manner, disdaining our antiquities and honourable customs? See now, the sachem's grave lies like the common people, defaced by an ignoble race. Thy mother

---

1 *The planters … piously decorated* See Morton's *New English Canaan*; the Sachem mentioned was the Massachusett leader Chickatawbut (d. 1633). The event—as well as Chickatawbut's speech—is also recorded in William Apess's *Eulogy on King Philip* (1836).
2 *tumulus* Grave mound.
3 *pathetic* Emotional; moving.

An instance of one of those sudden exasperations, arising from a motive peculiar to the Indian character, is extant in an old record of the early settlement of Massachusetts. The planters of Plymouth had defaced the monuments of the dead at Passonagessit, and had plundered the grave of the Sachem's mother of some skins with which it had been decorated. The Indians are remarkable for the reverence which they entertain for the sepulchres of their kindred. Tribes, that have passed generations exiled from the abodes of their ancestors, when by chance they have been travelling in the vicinity, have been known to turn aside from the highway, and, guided by wonderfully accurate tradition, have crossed the country for miles to some tumulus, buried perhaps in woods, where the bones of their tribe were anciently deposited; and there have passed hours in silent meditation. Influenced by this sublime and holy feeling, the Sachem, whose mother's tomb had been violated, gathered his men together, and addressed them in the following beautifully simple and pathetic harangue; a curious specimen of Indian eloquence, and an affecting instance of filial piety in a savage.

"When last the glorious light of all the sky was underneath this globe, and birds grew silent, I began to settle, as my custom is, to take repose. Before mine eyes were fast closed, methought I saw a vision, at which my spirit was much troubled; and, trembling at that doleful sight, a spirit cried aloud, 'Behold, my son, whom I have cherished, see the breasts that gave thee suck, the hands that lapped thee warm, and fed thee oft! Canst thou forget to take revenge of those wild people, who have defaced my monument in a despiteful manner, disdaining our antiquities and honourable customs. See now, the Sachem's grave lies like the common people, defaced by an ignoble race. Thy mother doth complain, and implores thy aid against this thievish people, who have newly intruded on our land. If this be suffered, I shall not rest quiet in my everlasting habitation.' This said, the spirit vanished, and I, all in a sweat, not able scarce to speak, began to get some strength, doth complain, and implores thy aid against this thievish people, who have newly intruded in our land. If this be suffered I shall not rest quiet in my everlasting habitation. This said, the spirit vanished, and I, all in a sweat, not able scarce to speak, began to get some strength and recollect my spirits that were fled, and determined to demand your counsel, and solicit your assistance."

Another cause of violent outcry against the Indians, is their inhumanity to the vanquished. This originally arose partly from political and partly from superstitious motives. Where hostile tribes are scanty in their numbers, the death of several warriors completely paralyzes their power; and many an instance occurs in Indian history, where a hostile tribe, that had long been formidable to its neighbour, has been broken up and driven away, by the capture and massacre of its principal fighting men. This is a strong temptation to the victor to be merciless, not so much to gratify any cruelty of revenge, as to provide for future security. But they had other motives, originating in a superstitious idea, common to barbarous nations, and even prevalent among the Greeks and Romans—that the manes of their deceased friends, slain in battle, were soothed by the blood of the captives. But those that are not thus sacrificed are adopted into their families, and treated with the confidence and affection of relatives and friends; nay, so hospitable and tender is their entertainment, that they will often prefer to remain with their adoptive brethren, rather than return to the home and the friends of their youth.

The inhumanity of the Indians towards their prisoners has been heightened since the intrusion of the whites. We have exasperated what was formerly a compliance with policy and superstition into a gratification of vengeance. They cannot but be sensible that we are the usurpers of their ancient dominion, the cause of their degradation, and the gradual destroyers of their race. They go forth to battle, smarting with injuries and indignities which they have individually suffered from the injustice and the arrogance of white men, and they are driven to madness and despair, by the wide-spreading desolation and recollect my spirits that were fled, and determined to demand your counsel and assistance."

I have adduced this anecdote at some length, as it tends to show, how these sudden acts of hostility, which have been attributed to caprice and perfidy, may often arise from deep and generous motives, which our inattention to Indian character and customs prevents our properly appreciating.

Another ground of violent outcry against the Indians is their barbarity to the vanquished. This had its origin partly in policy and partly in superstition. The tribes, though sometimes called nations, were never so formidable in their numbers, but that the loss of several warriors was sensibly felt; this was particularly the case when they had been frequently engaged in warfare; and many an instance occurs in Indian history, where a tribe that had long been formidable to its neighbours, has been broken up and driven away, by the capture and massacre of its principal fighting men. There was a strong temptation, therefore, to the victor to be merciless; not so much to gratify any cruel revenge, as to provide for future security. The Indians had also the superstitious belief, frequent among barbarous nations, and prevalent also among the ancients, that the manes of their friends who had fallen in battle, were soothed by the blood of the captives. The prisoners, however, who are not thus sacrifices, are adopted into their families in place of the slain, and are treated with the confidence and affection of relatives and friends; nay, so hospitable and tender is their entertainment, that when the alternative is offered them they will often prefer to remain with their adopted brethren, rather than return to the home and the friends of their youth.

The cruelty of the Indians towards their prisoners has been heightened since the colonization of the whites. What was formerly a compliance with policy and superstition has been exasperated into a gratification of vengeance. They cannot but be sensible that the white men are the usurpers of their ancient dominion, the cause of their degradation, and the gradual destroyers of their race. They go forth to battle, smarting with injuries and indignities which they have individually suffered, and they are driven to madness and despair by the wide-spreading desolation, and the overwhelming ruin of Euro-

and the overwhelming ruin of our warfare. We set them an example of violence, by burning their villages and laying waste their slender means of subsistence; and then wonder that savages will not show moderation and magnanimity towards men, who have left them nothing but mere existence and wretchedness.

It is a common thing to exclaim against new forms of cruelty, while, reconciled by custom, we wink at long-established atrocities. What right does the generosity of our conduct give us to rail exclusively at Indian warfare? With all the doctrines of Christianity, and the advantages of cultivated morals, to govern and direct us, what horrid crimes disgrace the victories of Christian armies? Towns laid in ashes; cities given up to the sword; enormities perpetrated, at which manhood blushes, and history drops the pen. Well may we exclaim at the outrages of the scalping knife; but where, in the records of Indian barbarity, can we point to a violated female?

We stigmatize the Indians also as cowardly and treacherous, because they use stratagem in warfare, in preference to open force; but in this they are fully authorized by their rude[1] code of honour. They are early taught that stratagem is praiseworthy; the bravest warrior thinks it no disgrace to lurk in silence and take every advantage of his foe. He triumphs in the superior craft and sagacity by which he has been enabled to surprise and massacre an enemy. Indeed, man is naturally more prone to subtlety than open valour, owing to his physical weakness in comparison with other animals. They are endowed with natural weapons of defence; with horns, with tusks, with hoofs and talons; but man has to depend on his superior sagacity. In all his encounters, therefore, with these, his proper enemies, he has to resort to stratagem; and when he perversely turns his hostility against his fellow man, he continues the same subtle mode of warfare.

The natural principle of war is to do the most harm to our enemy, with the least harm to ourselves; and this of course is to be effected by cunning. That chivalric kind of courage which teaches us to despise the suggestions of prudence, and to rush in the face of certain danger, is the offspring of society, and produced by education. It is honour-

---

1   *rude* Simple; uncultivated.

pean warfare. The whites have too frequently set them an example of violence, by burning their villages and laying waste their slender means of subsistence; and yet they wonder that savages do not show moderation and magnanimity towards those, who have left them nothing but mere existence and wretchedness.

We stigmatize the Indians, also, as cowardly and treacherous, because they use stratagem in warfare, in preference to open force; but in this they are fully justified by their rude code of honour. They are early taught that stratagem is praiseworthy; the bravest warrior thinks it no disgrace to lurk in silence, and take every advantage of his foe; he triumphs in the superior craft and sagacity by which he has been enabled to surprize and destroy an enemy. Indeed man is naturally more prone to subtlety than open valour, owing to his physical weakness in comparison with other animals. They are endowed with natural weapons of defence; with horns, with tusks, with hoofs and talons; but man has to depend on his superior sagacity. In all his encounters with these, his proper enemies, he resorts to stratagem; and when he perversely turns his hostility against his fellow-man, he at first continues the same subtle mode of warfare.

The natural principle of war is to do the most harm to our enemy with the least harm to ourselves; and this of course is to be effected by stratagem. That chivalrous courage which induces us to despise the suggestions of prudence, and to rush in the face of certain danger, is the offspring of society, and produced by education. It is honourable, because it is in fact the triumph of lofty sentiment over an instinctive repugnance to pain, and over those yearnings after personal ease and

able, because in fact it is the triumph of lofty sentiment over an instinctive repugnance to pain, and over those selfish yearnings after personal ease and security which society has condemned as ignoble. It is an emotion kept up by pride, and the fear of shame; and thus the dread of real evils is overcome by the superior dread of an evil that exists but in the mind. This may be instanced in the case of a young British officer of great pride, but delicate nerves, who was going for the first time into battle. Being agitated by the novelty and awful peril of the scene, he was accosted by another officer of a rough and boisterous character—"What, Sir," cried he, "do you tremble?" "Yes Sir," replied the other, "and if you were half as much afraid as I am you would run away." This young officer signalized himself on many occasions by his gallantry, though, had he been brought up in savage life, or even in a humbler and less responsible situation, it is more probable he could never have ventured into open action.

Besides we must consider how much the quality of open and desperate courage is cherished and stimulated by society. It has been the theme of many a spirit-stirring song, and chivalric story. The minstrel has sung of it to the loftiest strain of his lyre—the poet has delighted to shed around it all the splendours of fiction—and even the historian has forgotten the sober gravity of narration, and burst forth into enthusiasm and rhapsody in its praise. Triumphs and gorgeous pageants have been its reward—monuments, where art has exhausted its skill, and opulence its treasures, have been erected to perpetuate a nation's gratitude and admiration. Thus artificially excited, courage has arisen to an extraordinary and factitious degree of heroism; and, arrayed in all the glorious "pomp and circumstance" of war,[1] this turbulent quality has even been able to eclipse many of those quiet, but invaluable virtues, which silently ennoble the human character, and swell the tide of human happiness.

But if courage intrinsically consist in the defiance of danger and pain, the life of the Indian is a continual exhibition of it. He lives in a perpetual state of hostility and risk. Peril and adventure are congenial to

---

1   *"pomp and circumstance" of war*   See Shakespeare's *Othello* 3.3.406: "Pride, pomp, and circumstance of glorious war!"

security, which society has condemned as ignoble. It is kept alive by pride and the fear of shame; and thus the dread of real evil is overcome by the superior dread of an evil which exists but in the imagination. It has been cherished and stimulated also by various means. It has been the theme of spirit-stirring song and chivalrous story. The poet and minstrel have delighted to shed round it the splendours of fiction; and even the historian has forgotten the sober gravity of narration, and broken forth into enthusiasm and rhapsody in its praise. Triumphs and gorgeous pageants have been its reward: monuments, on which art has exhausted its skill, and opulence its treasures, have been erected to perpetuate a nation's gratitude and admiration. Thus artificially excited, courage has arisen to an extraordinary and factitious degree of heroism; and, arrayed in all the glorious "pomp and circumstance of war," this turbulent quality has even been able to eclipse many of those quiet, but invaluable virtues, which silently ennoble the human character, and swell the tide of human happiness.

But if courage intrinsically consists in the defiance of danger and pain, the life of the Indian is a continual exhibition of it. He lives in a state of perpetual hostility and risk. Peril and adventure are congenial to his nature; or rather seem necessary to arouse his faculties and to give an interest to his existence. Surrounded by hostile tribes, whose mode of warfare is by ambush and surprisal, he is always prepared for

his nature, or, rather, seem necessary to arouse his faculties and give an interest to existence. Surrounded by hostile tribes, he is always equipped for fight, with his weapons in his hands. He traverses vast wildernesses, exposed to the hazards of lonely sickness, of lurking enemies, or pining famine. Stormy lakes present no obstacle to his wanderings; in his light canoe of bark, he sports like a feather on their waves, and darts with the swiftness of an arrow down the roaring rapids of the rivers. Trackless wastes of snow, rugged mountains, the glooms of swamps and morasses, where poisonous reptiles curl among the rank vegetation, are fearlessly encountered by this wanderer of the wilderness. He gains his food by the hardships and dangers of the chase; he wraps himself in the spoils of the bear, the panther, and the buffalo, and sleeps among the thunders of the cataract.

No hero of ancient or modern days can surpass the Indian in his lofty contempt of death, and the fortitude with which he sustains all the varied torments with which it is frequently inflicted. Indeed, we here behold him rising superior to the white man, merely in consequence of his peculiar education. The latter rushes to glorious death at the cannon's mouth; the former coolly contemplates its approach, and triumphantly endures it, amid the torments of the knife and the protracted agonies of fire. He even takes a savage delight in taunting his persecutors, and provoking their ingenuity of torture; and as the devouring flames prey on his very vitals, and the flesh shrinks from the sinews, he raises his last song of triumph, breathing the defiance of an unconquered heart, and invoking the spirits of his fathers to witness that he dies without a groan.

Notwithstanding all the obloquy with which the early historians of the colonies have overshadowed the characters of the unfortunate natives, some bright gleams will occasionally break through, that throw a degree of melancholy lustre on their memories. Facts are occasionally to be met with, in their rude annals, which, though recorded with all the colouring of prejudice and bigotry, yet speak for themselves, and will be dwelt on with applause and sympathy, when prejudice shall have passed away.

fight, and lives with his weapons in his hands. As the ship careers in fearful singleness through the solitudes of ocean—as the bird mingles among clouds, and storms, and wings its way, a mere speck, across the pathless fields of air—so the Indian holds his course, silent, solitary, but undaunted, through the boundless bosom of the wilderness. His expeditions may vie in distance and danger with the pilgrimage of the devotee, or the crusade of the knight-errant. He traverses vast forests, exposed to the hazards of lonely sickness, of lurking enemies and pining famine. Stormy lakes, those great inland seas, are no obstacles to his wanderings: in his light canoe of bark he sports, like a feather, on their waves, and darts, with the swiftness of an arrow, down the roaring rapids of the river. His very subsistence is snatched from the midst of toil and peril. He gains his food by the hardships and dangers of the chase; he wraps himself in the spoils of the bear, the panther, and the buffalo, and sleeps among the thunders of the cataract.

No hero of ancient or modern days can surpass the Indian in his lofty contempt of death, and the fortitude with which he sustains its cruelest infliction. Indeed we here behold him rising superior to the white man, in consequence of his peculiar education. The latter rushes to glorious death at the cannon's mouth; the former calmly contemplates its approach, and triumphantly endures it, amidst the varied torments of surrounding foes and the protracted agonies of fire. He even takes a pride in taunting his persecutors, and provoking their ingenuity of torture; and as the devouring flames prey on his very vitals, and the flesh shrinks from the sinews, he raises his last song of triumph, breathing the defiance of an unconquered heart, and invoking the spirits of his fathers to witness that he dies without a groan.

Notwithstanding the obloquy with which the early historians have overshadowed the characters of the unfortunate natives, some bright gleams occasionally break through, which throw a degree of melancholy lustre on their memories. Facts are occasionally to be met with in the rude annals of the eastern provinces, which, though recorded with the colouring of prejudice and bigotry, yet speak for themselves; and will be dwelt on with applause and sympathy, when prejudice shall have passed away.

In one of the homely narratives of the Indian wars in New England there is a touching account of the desolation carried into the tribe of the Pequod Indians. Humanity shudders at the cold-blooded accounts given, of indiscriminate butchery on the part of the settlers. In one place we read of the surprisal of an Indian fort in the night, when the wigwams were wrapped in flames, and the miserable inhabitants shot down and slain, in attempting to escape, "all being despatched and ended in the course of an hour."[1] After a series of similar transactions, "Our soldiers," as the historian piously observes, "being resolved by God's assistance to make a final destruction of them," the unhappy savages being hunted from their homes and fortresses, and pursued with fire and sword, a scanty but gallant band, the sad remnant of the Pequod warriors, with their wives and children, took refuge in a swamp.

Burning with indignation, and rendered sullen by despair—with hearts bursting with grief at the destruction of their tribe, and spirits galled and sore at the fancied ignominy of their defeat, they refused to ask their lives at the hands of an insulting foe, and preferred death to submission.

As the night drew on they were surrounded in their dismal retreat, in such manner as to render escape impracticable. Thus situated, their enemy "plied them with shot all the time, by which means many were killed and buried in the mire." In the darkness and fog that precedes the dawn of day, some few broke through the besiegers and escaped into the woods: "the rest were left to the conquerors, of which many were killed in the swamp, like sullen dogs who would rather, in their self willedness and madness, sit still and be shot through, or cut to pieces," than implore for mercy. When the day broke upon this handful of forlorn but dauntless spirits, the soldiers, we are told, entering the swamp, "saw several heaps of them sitting close together, upon whom they discharged their pieces, laden with ten or twelve pistol bullets at a time; putting the muzzles of their pieces under the boughs, within a few yards of them; so as, besides those that were

---

1   *all being ... an hour*   The source of the information and quotations in the following section is William Hubbard's *A Narrative of the Indian Wars in New-England* (1677).

In one of the homely narratives of the Indian wars in New England, there is a touching account of the desolation carried into the tribe of the Pequod Indians. Humanity shrinks from the cold-blooded detail of indiscriminate butchery. In one place we read of the surprisal of an Indian fort in the night, when the wigwams were wrapped in flames, and the miserable inhabitants shot down and slain in attempting to escape, "all being dispatched and ended in the course of an hour." After a series of similar transactions, "our soldiers," as the historian piously observes, "being resolved by God's assistance to make a final destruction of them," the unhappy savages being hunted from their homes and fortresses, and pursued with fire and sword, a scanty but gallant band, the sad remnant of the Pequod warriors, with their wives and children, took refuge in a swamp.

Burning with indignation, and rendered sullen by despair, with hearts bursting with grief at the destruction of their tribe, and spirits galled and sore at the fancied ignominy of their defeat, they refused to ask their lives at the hands of an insulting foe, and preferred death to submission.

As the night drew on, they were surrounded in their dismal retreat, so as to render escape impracticable. Thus situated, their enemy "plied them with shot all the time, by which means many were killed and buried in the mire." In the darkness and fog that preceded the dawn of day some few broke through the besiegers and escaped into the woods: "the rest were left to the conquerors, of which many were killed in the swamp, like sullen dogs who would rather, in their self-willedness and madness, sit still and be shot through, or cut to pieces," than implore for mercy. When the day broke upon this handful of forlorn but dauntless spirits, the soldiers, we are told, entering the swamp, "saw several heaps of them sitting close together, upon whom they discharged their pieces, laden with ten or twelve pistol bullets at a time; putting the muzzles of their pieces under the boughs, within a few yards of them; so as, besides those that were found dead, many more were killed and sunk into the mire, and never were minded more by friend or foe."

found dead, many more were killed and sunk into the mire, and never were minded more by friend or foe."

Can any one read this plain unvarnished tale,[1] without admiring the stern resolution, the unbending pride, and loftiness of spirit, that seemed to nerve the hearts of these self-taught heroes, and to raise them above the instinctive feelings of human nature? When the Gauls laid waste the city of Rome, they found the nobles clothed in their robes, and seated with stern tranquillity in their curule chairs; in this manner they suffered death without an attempt at supplication or resistance.[2] Such conduct in them was applauded as noble and magnanimous; in the hapless Indian it was reviled as obstinate and sullen. How much are we the dupes of show and circumstance! How different is virtue, arrayed in purple and enthroned in state, from virtue, destitute and naked, reduced to the last stage of wretchedness, and perishing obscurely in a wilderness.

Do these records of ancient excesses fill us with disgust and aversion? Let us take heed that we do not suffer ourselves to be hurried into the same iniquities. Posterity lifts up its hands with horror at past misdeeds, because the passions that urged to them are not felt, and the arguments that persuaded to them are forgotten; but we are reconciled to the present perpetration of injustice by all the selfish motives with which interest chills the heart and silences the conscience. Even at the present advanced day, when we should suppose that enlightened philosophy had expanded our minds, and true religion had warmed our hearts into philanthropy—when we have been admonished by a sense of past transgressions, and instructed by the indignant censures of candid history—even now, we perceive a disposition breaking out to renew the persecutions of these hapless beings. Sober-thoughted men, far from the scenes of danger, in the security of cities and populous regions, can coolly talk of "exterminating measures," and discuss

---

1   *plain unvarnished tale*   See Shakespeare's *Othello* 1.3.106: "I will a round unvarnished tale deliver."

2   *When the Gauls ... or resistance*   Irving refers to the Gallic sack of the Roman Republic c. 390 BCE. The Gauls were composed of various groups of Celtic peoples who inhabited a region in West-Central Europe known as Gaul;   *curule chairs*   Chairs used by the most senior magistrates of the Roman Republic.

Can any one read this plain unvarnished tale, without admiring the stern resolution, the unbending pride, the loftiness of spirit, that seemed to nerve the hearts of these self-taught heroes, and to raise them above the instinctive feelings of human nature? When the Gauls laid waste the city of Rome, they found the senators clothed in their robes and seated with stern tranquillity in their curule chairs; in this manner they suffered death without resistance or even supplication. Such conduct was, in them, applauded as noble and magnanimous; in the hapless Indian it was reviled as obstinate and sullen. How truly are we the dupes of show and circumstance! How different is virtue, clothed in purple and enthroned in state, from virtue naked and destitute, and perishing obscurely in a wilderness.

the *policy* of extirpating thousands. If such is the talk in the cities, what is the temper displayed on the borders? The sentence of desolation has gone forth—"the roar is up amidst the woods";[1] implacable wrath, goaded on by interest and prejudice, is ready to confound all rights, to trample on all claims of justice and humanity, and to act over those scenes of sanguinary vengeance which have too often stained the pages of colonial history.

These are not the idle suggestions of fancy; they are wrung forth by recent facts, which still haunt the public mind. We need but turn to the ravaged country of the Creeks to behold a picture of exterminating warfare.

These deluded savages, either excited by private injury or private intrigue, or by both, have lately taken up the hatchet and made deadly inroads into our frontier settlements. Their punishment has been pitiless and terrible. Vengeance has gone like a devouring fire through their country—the smoke of their villages yet rises to heaven, and the blood of the slaughtered Indians yet reeks upon the earth. Of this merciless ravage, an idea may be formed by a single exploit, boastfully set forth in an official letter that has darkened our public journals.[2] A detachment of soldiery had been sent under the command of one General Coffee to destroy the Tallushatches towns, where the hostile Creeks had assembled. The enterprise was executed, as the commander in chief[3] expresses it, *in style*—but, in the name of mercy, in what style! The towns were surrounded before the break of day. The inhabitants, starting from their sleep, flew to arms, with beat of drums and hideous yellings. The soldiery pressed upon them on every side, and met with a desperate resistance—but what was savage valour against the array and discipline of scientific warfare? The Creeks made gallant charges, but were beaten back by overwhelming numbers. Hemmed in like savage beasts surrounded by the hunters, wherever they turned they met a foe, and in every foe they found a butcher. "The enemy retreated firing," says Coffee in his letter, "until they got

---

1 *the roar ... the woods* See John Milton's *Comus* (1634), lines 549–50: "The wonted roar was up amidst the Woods, / And fill'd the Air with barbarous dissonance."

2 [Irving's note] Letter of Gen. Coffee, dated Nov. 4, 1813.

3 [Irving's note] General Andrew Jackson.

around and in their buildings, where they made all the resistance that an overpowered soldier could do; they fought as long as one existed, but their destruction was very soon completed; our men rushed up to the doors of the houses, and in a few minutes killed the last warrior of them; the enemy fought with savage fury, and met death with all its horrors, without shrinking or complaining; not one asked to be spared, but fought so long as they could stand or sit. In consequence of their flying to their houses, and mixing with the families, our men in killing the males, without intention, *killed and wounded a few of the squaws and children.*"

So unsparing was the carnage of the sword, that not one of the warriors escaped to carry the heart-breaking tidings to the remainder of the tribe. Such is what is termed executing hostilities *in style*! Let those who exclaim with abhorrence at Indian inroads—those who are so eloquent about the bitterness of Indian recrimination—let them turn to the horrible victory of General Coffee, and be silent.

As yet our government has in some measure restrained the tide of vengeance, and inculcated lenity towards the hapless Indians who have been duped into the present war. Such temper is worthy of an enlightened government—let it still be observed—let sharp rebuke and signal punishment be inflicted on those who abuse their delegated power, and disgrace their victories with massacre and conflagration. The enormities of the Indians form no excuse for the enormities of white men. It has pleased heaven to give them but limited powers of mind, and feeble lights to guide their judgments; it becomes us who are blessed with higher intellects to think for them, and to set them an example of humanity. It is the nature of vengeance, if unrestrained, to be headlong in its actions, and to lay up, in a moment of passion, ample cause for an age's repentance. We may roll over these miserable beings with our chariot wheels, and crush them to the earth; but when war has done its worst—when passion has subsided, and it is too late to pity or to save—we shall look back with unavailing compunction at the mangled corpses of those whose cries were unheeded in the fury of our career.

Let the fate of war go as it may, the fate of those ignorant tribes that have been inveigled from their forests to mingle in the strife of

[*1820 version*]

white men, will be inevitably the same. In the collision of two powerful nations, these intervening particles of population will be crumbled to dust, and scattered to the winds of heaven. In a little while, and they will go the way that so many tribes have gone before. The few hordes that still linger about the shores of Huron and Superior, and the tributary streams of the Mississippi, will share the fate of those tribes that once lorded it along the proud banks of the Hudson; of that gigantic race that are said to have existed on the borders of the Susquehanna, and of those various nations that flourished about the Potomac and the Rappahannock, and that peopled the forests of the vast valley Shenandoah. They will vanish like a vapour from the face of the earth—their very history will be lost in forgetfulness—and "the places that now know them will know them no more forever."

Or if perchance some dubious memorial of them should survive the lapse of time, it may be in the romantic dreams of the poet, to populate in imagination his glades and groves, like the fauns, and satyrs, and sylvan deities[1] of antiquity. But should he venture upon the dark story of their wrongs and wretchedness—should he tell how they were invaded, corrupted, despoiled—driven from their native abodes and the sepulchres of their fathers—hunted like wild beasts about the earth, and sent down in violence and butchery to the grave—posterity will either turn with horror and incredulity from the tale, or blush with indignation at the inhumanity of their forefathers. "We are driven back," said an old warrior, "until we can retreat no further—our hatchets are broken—our bows are snapped—our fires are nearly extinguished—a little longer and the white men will cease to persecute us—for we will cease to exist!"[2]

—1814

---

1   *fauns, and satyrs, and sylvan deities*   Various woodland deities of Classical mythology.
2   *We are … to exist!*   The source of the quotation is unknown.

But I forbear to dwell upon these gloomy pictures. The eastern tribes have long since disappeared; the forests that sheltered them have been laid low, and scarce any trees remain of them in the thickly settled states of New England, excepting here and there the Indian name of a village or a stream. And such must sooner or later be the fate of those other tribes which skirt the frontiers, and have occasionally been inveigled from their forests to mingle in the wars of white men. In a little while, and they will go the way that their brethren have gone before. The few hordes which still linger about the shores of Huron and Superior, and the tributary streams of the Mississippi, will share the fate of those tribes that once spread over Massachusetts and Connecticut, and lorded it along the proud banks of the Hudson; of that gigantic race said to have existed on the borders of the Susquehanna; and of those various nations that flourished about the Potomac and the Rappahannock, and that peopled the forests of the vast valley of Shenandoah. They will vanish like a vapour from the face of the earth; their very history will be lost in forgetfulness; and "the places that now know them will know them no more forever." Or if, perchance, some dubious memorial of them should survive the lapse of time, it may be in the romantic dreams of the poet, to people in imagination his glades and groves, like the fauns and satyrs and sylvan deities of antiquity. But should he venture upon the dark story of their wrongs and wretchedness; should he tell how they were invaded, corrupted, despoiled; driven from their native abodes and the sepulchres of their fathers; hunted like wild beasts about the earth; and sent down with violence and butchery to the grave; posterity will either turn with horror and incredulity from the tale, or blush with indignation at the inhumanity of their forefathers. "We are driven back," said an old warrior, "until we can retreat no further—our hatchets are broken, our bows are snapped, our fires are nearly extinguished—a little longer and the white man will cease to persecute us—for we shall cease to exist!"
—1820

The Legend of Sleepy Hollow

(Found Among the Papers of the Late Diedrich Knickerbocker.)

> A pleasing land of drowsy head it was,
> Of dreams that wave before the half-shut eye;
> And of gay castles in the clouds that pass,
> Forever flushing round a summer sky.
> CASTLE OF INDOLENCE[1]

In the bosom of one of those spacious coves which indent the eastern shore of the Hudson, at that broad expansion of the river denominated by the ancient Dutch navigators the Tappaan Zee,[2] and where they always prudently shortened sail, and implored the protection of St. Nicholas[3] when they crossed, there lies a small market town or rural port, which by some is called Greensburg, but which is more universally and properly known by the name of Tarry Town. This name was given, we are told, in former days, by the good housewives of the adjacent country, from the inveterate propensity of their husbands to linger about the village tavern on market days. Be that as it may, I do not vouch for the fact, but merely advert to it, for the sake of being precise and authentic. Not far from this village, perhaps about three miles, there is a little valley, or rather lap of land among high hills, which is one of the quietest places in the whole world. A small brook glides through it, with just murmur enough to lull you to repose, and the occasional whistle of a quail, or tapping of a woodpecker, is almost the only sound that ever breaks in upon the uniform tranquillity.

I recollect that, when a stripling,[4] my first exploit in squirrel shooting was in a grove of tall walnut trees that shades one side of the valley. I had wandered into it at noon time, when all nature is pecu-

---

1   CASTLE OF INDOLENCE   1748 poem by Scottish writer James Thomson.
2   *that broad expansion ... Tappaan Zee*   Irving refers to the natural widening of the Hudson River in southeastern New York, named the Tappaan Zee by navigators for the Dutch East India Company (including the English explorer Henry Hudson) in the early 1600s.
3   *St. Nicholas*   Patron saint of Amsterdam.
4   *stripling*   Youth.

liarly quiet, and was startled by the roar of my own gun, as it broke the sabbath stillness around, and was prolonged and reverberated by the angry echoes. If ever I should wish for a retreat, whither I might steal from the world and its distractions, and dream quietly away the remnant of a troubled life, I know of none more promising than this little valley.

From the listless repose of the place, and the peculiar character of its inhabitants, who are descendants from the original Dutch settlers, this sequestered glen has long been known by the name of Sleepy Hollow, and its rustic lads are called the Sleepy Hollow Boys throughout all the neighbouring country. A drowsy, dreamy influence seems to hang over the land, and pervade the very atmosphere. Some say that the place was bewitched by a high German[1] doctor during the early days of the settlement; others, that an old Indian chief, the prophet or wizard of his tribe, held his powwows there before the country was discovered by Master Hendrick Hudson. Certain it is, the place still continues under the sway of some witching power, that holds a spell over the minds of the good people, causing them to walk in a continual reverie. They are given to all kinds of marvellous beliefs; have trances and visions, and see strange sights, and hear music and voices in the air. The whole neighbourhood abounds with local tales, haunted spots, and twilight superstitions; stars shoot and meteors glare oftener across the valley than in any other part of the country, and the nightmare, with her whole nine fold,[2] seems to make it the favourite scene of her gambols.

The dominant spirit, however, that haunts this enchanted region, and seems to be commander of all the powers of the air, is the apparition of a figure on horseback without a head. It is said by some to be the ghost of a Hessian[3] trooper, whose head had been carried away by a cannon-ball, in some nameless battle during the revolutionary war, and who is ever and anon seen by various of the country people, hurrying along in the gloom of night, as if on the wings of the wind.

---

1 *high German* From the mountainous southern region of Germany.

2 *nightmare … nine fold* See Shakespeare's *King Lear* 3.4.116–18. "Nightmare" originally referred to a demonic creature from Slavic and Germanic folklore; in this scene in *King Lear*, the demon is envisioned as a female with nine children.

3 *Hessian* German soldier hired by the British Army to fight against the revolutionaries during the American Revolution.

His haunts are not confined to the valley, but extend at times to the adjacent roads, and especially to the vicinity of a church that is at no great distance. Indeed, certain of the most authentic historians of those parts, who have been careful in collecting and collating the floating facts concerning this spectre, allege, that the body of the trooper having been buried in the churchyard, the ghost rides forth to the scene of battle in nightly quest of his head, and the rushing speed with which he sometimes passes along the hollow, like a midnight blast, is owing to his being belated, and in a hurry to get back to the churchyard before daybreak.

Such is the general purport of this legendary superstition, which has furnished materials for many a wild story in that region of shadows; and the spectre is known, at all the country firesides, by the name of The Headless Horseman of Sleepy Hollow.

It is remarkable, that the visionary turn I have mentioned is not confined to the native inhabitants of the valley, but is imperceptibly acquired by everyone who resides there for a time. However wide awake they may have been before they entered that sleepy region, they are sure, in a little time, to imbibe the witching influence of the air, and begin to grow imaginative—to dream dreams, and see apparitions.

I mention this peaceful spot with all possible laud; for it is in such little retired Dutch valleys, found here and there embosomed in the great state of New York, that populations, manners, and customs, remain fixed, while the great torrent of emigration and improvement, which is making such incessant changes in other parts of this restless country, sweeps by them unobserved. They are like those little nooks of still water, which border a rapid stream, where we may see the straw and bubble riding quietly at anchor, or slowly revolving in their mimic harbour, undisturbed by the rushing of the passing current. Though many years have elapsed since I trod the drowsy shades of Sleepy Hollow, yet I question whether I should not still find the same trees and the same families vegetating in its sheltered bosom.

In this by-place of nature there abode, in a remote period of American history, that is to say, some thirty years since, a worthy wight[1] of the name of Ichabod Crane, who sojourned, or, as he

---

1 *wight* Person.

expressed it, "tarried," in Sleepy Hollow, for the purpose of instructing the children of the vicinity. He was a native of Connecticut, a
state which supplies the Union with pioneers for the mind as well
as the forest, and sends forth yearly its legions of frontier wood-
men and country schoolmasters. The cognomen of Crane was not
inapplicable to his person.[1] He was tall, but exceedingly lank, with
narrow shoulders, long arms and legs, hands that dangled a mile
out of his sleeves, feet that might have served for shovels, and his
whole frame most loosely hung together. His head was small, and
flat at top, with huge ears, large green glassy eyes, and a long snipe
nose, so that it might have been mistaken for a weathercock perched
upon his spindle neck, to tell which way the wind blew. To see him
striding along the profile of a hill on a windy day, with his clothes
bagging and fluttering about him, one might have mistaken him for
the genius of famine[2] descending upon the earth, or some scarecrow
eloped from a cornfield.

His schoolhouse was a low building of one large room, rudely
constructed of logs; the windows partly glazed, and partly patched
with leaves of old copy books. It was most ingeniously secured at
vacant hours, by a withe[3] twisted in the handle of the door, and stakes
set against the window shutters; so that though a thief might get in
with perfect ease, he would find some embarrassment in getting out;
an idea most probably borrowed by the architect, Yost Van Houten,
from the mystery of an eelpot.[4] The schoolhouse stood in rather a
lonely but a pleasant situation, just at the foot of a woody hill, with
a brook running close by, and a formidable birch tree growing at one
end of it. From hence the low murmur of his pupils' voices conning[5]
over their lessons, might be heard of a drowsy summer's day, like the
hum of a bee-hive; interrupted now and then by the authoritative
voice of the master, giving menace or command, or, peradventure, the
appalling sound of the birch, as he urged some tardy loiterer along the
flowery path of knowledge. Truth to say, he was a conscientious man,

---

1 *The cognomen ... his person* I.e., the surname Crane served as an accurate descriptor of his
physical appearance.
2 *genius of famine* See Shakespeare's *2 Henry IV* 3.2.325; *genius* Spirit; essence.
3 *withe* Strong, flexible branch, as from a willow tree, used to tie something in place.
4 *eelpot* Basket for trapping eels.
5 *conning* Poring over; studying.

that ever bore in mind the golden maxim, "spare the rod and spoil the child."[1] Ichabod Crane's scholars certainly were not spoiled.

I would not have it imagined, however, that he was one of those cruel potentates of the school, who joy in the smart[2] of their subjects; on the contrary, he administered justice with discrimination rather than severity; taking the burden off the backs of the weak, and laying it on those of the strong. Your mere puny stripling, that winced at the least flourish of the rod, was passed by with indulgence; but the claims of justice were satisfied, by giving a double portion to some little, tough, wrong-headed, broad-skirted Dutch urchin, who sulked and swelled and grew dogged and sullen beneath the birch. All this he called "doing his duty by their parents"; and he never inflicted a chastisement without following it by the assurance, so consolatory to the smarting urchin, that he would remember it and thank him for it the longest day he had to live.

When school hours were over, he was even the companion and playmate of his larger boys; and would convoy some of the smaller ones home of a holiday, who happened to have pretty sisters, or good housewives for mothers, noted for the comforts of the cupboard. Indeed, it behooved him to keep on good terms with his pupils. The revenue arising from his school was small, and would have been scarcely sufficient to furnish him with daily bread, for he was a huge feeder, and though lank, had the dilating powers of an anaconda; but to help out his maintenance, he was, according to country custom in those parts, boarded and lodged at the houses of the farmers, whose children he instructed. With these he lived alternately a week at a time, thus going the rounds of the neighbourhood, with all his worldly effects tied up in a cotton handkerchief.

That all this might not be too onerous on the purses of his rustic patrons, who are apt to consider the costs of schooling a grievous burden, and schoolmasters mere drones,[3] he had various ways of rendering himself both useful and agreeable. He assisted the farmers occasionally in the light labours of their farms, helped to make

---

1 *spare the ... the child* See Proverbs 13.24: "He that spareth his rod hateth his son: but he that loveth him chasteneth him betimes."

2 *smart* Sting; pain.

3 *drones* Male bees, who do no work except mate with the queen bee; in other words, idle and lazy people.

hay, mended the fences, took the horses to water, drove the cows from pasture, and cut wood for the winter fire. He laid aside, too, all the dominant dignity and absolute sway, with which he lorded it in his little empire, the school, and became wonderfully gentle and ingratiating. He found favour in the eyes of the mothers, by petting the children, particularly the youngest, and like the lion bold, which whilome so magnanimously the lamb did hold,[1] he would sit with a child on one knee, and rock a cradle with his foot, for whole hours together.

In addition to his other vocations, he was the singing-master of the neighbourhood, and picked up many bright shillings by instructing the young folks in psalmody. It was a matter of no little vanity to him on Sundays, to take his station in front of the church gallery, with a band of chosen singers; where, in his own mind, he completely carried away the palm[2] from the parson. Certain it is, his voice resounded far above all the rest of the congregation, and there are peculiar quavers still to be heard in that church, and which may even be heard half-a-mile off, quite to the opposite side of the mill-pond, of a still Sunday morning, which are said to be legitimately descended from the nose of Ichabod Crane. Thus, by diverse little make shifts, in that ingenious way which is commonly denominated "by hook and by crook,"[3] the worthy pedagogue got on tolerably enough, and was thought, by all those who understood nothing of the labour of headwork, to have a wonderful easy life of it.

The schoolmaster is generally a man of some importance in the female circle of a rural neighbourhood, being considered a kind of idle gentleman-like personage, of vastly superior taste and accomplishments to the rough country swains, and, indeed, inferior in learning only to the parson. His appearance, therefore, is apt to occasion some little stir at the tea-table of a farmhouse, and the addition of a supernumerary dish of cakes or sweetmeats, or, peradventure, the parade of a silver teapot. Our man of letters, therefore, was peculiarly happy in the smiles of all the country damsels. How he would

---

1 *the lion bold ... the lamb did hold* Allusion to the verse illustrating the letter "L" in the *New-England Primer*, a widely used seventeenth-century schoolbook; *whilome* In a time past.

2 *palm* Referring to the palm frond as a symbol of triumph or excellence.

3 *by hook and by crook* By one means or another.

figure among them in the churchyard, between services on Sundays; gathering grapes for them from the wild vines that overrun the surrounding trees; reciting for them all the epitaphs on the tomb-stones, or sauntering, with a whole bevy of them, along the banks of the adjacent mill-pond; while the more bashful country bumpkins hung sheepishly back, envying his superior elegance and address.

From his half itinerant life, also, he was a kind of travelling gazette, carrying the whole budget of local gossip from house to house; so that his appearance was always greeted with satisfaction. He was, moreover, esteemed by the women as a man of great erudition, for he had read several books quite through, and was a perfect master of Cotton Mather's[1] History of New-England Witchcraft, in which, by the way, he most firmly and potently believed.

He was, in fact, an odd mixture of small shrewdness and simple credulity. His appetite for the marvellous, and his powers of digesting it, were equally extraordinary; and both had been increased by his residence in this spellbound region. No tale was too gross or monstrous for his capacious swallow. It was often his delight, after his school was dismissed of an afternoon, to stretch himself on the rich bed of clover, bordering the little brook that whimpered past his schoolhouse, and there con over old Mather's direful tales, until the gathering dusk of evening made the printed page a mere mist before his eyes. Then, as he wended his way, by swamp and stream and awful woodland, to the farmhouse where he happened to be quartered, every sound of nature, at that witching hour, fluttered his excited imagination: the moan of the whip-poor-will[2] from the hill side; the boding cry of the tree-toad, that harbinger of storm; the dreary hooting of the screech-owl; or the sudden rustling in the thicket, of birds frightened from their roost. The fireflies, too, which sparkled most vividly in the darkest places, now and then startled him, as one of uncommon brightness would stream across his path; and if, by chance, a huge blockhead of a beetle came winging his blundering flight against him, the poor

---

1   *Cotton Mather*   Influential Puritan minister (1663–1728) from Massachusetts, known in large part for his involvement in the Salem witch trials; though Mather did write on witchcraft, the title Irving gives is erroneous.

2   *whip-poor-will*   Irving provides a footnote for this American species in the London edition of *The Sketch Book*: "The whip-poor-will is a bird which is only heard at night. It receives its name from its note, which is thought to resemble those words."

varlet was ready to give up the ghost, with the idea that he was struck with a witch's token. His only resource on such occasions, either to drown thought, or drive away evil spirits, was to sing psalm tunes; and the good people of Sleepy Hollow, as they sat by their doors of an evening, were often filled with awe, at hearing his nasal melody, "in linked sweetness long drawn out,"[1] floating from the distant hill, or along the dusky road.

Another of his sources of fearful pleasure was, to pass long winter evenings with the old Dutch wives, as they sat spinning by the fire, with a row of apples roasting and spluttering along the hearth, and listen to their marvellous tales of ghosts and goblins, and haunted fields and haunted brooks, and haunted bridges and haunted houses, and particularly of the headless horseman, or galloping Hessian of the Hollow, as they sometimes called him. He would delight them equally by his anecdotes of witchcraft, and of the direful omens and portentous sights and sounds in the air, which prevailed in the earlier times of Connecticut; and would frighten them woefully with speculations upon comets and shooting stars, and with the alarming fact that the world did absolutely turn round, and that they were half the time topsy-turvy!

But if there was a pleasure in all this, while snugly cuddling in the chimney corner of a chamber that was all of a ruddy glow from the crackling wood fire, and where, of course, no spectre dare to show its face, it was dearly purchased by the terrors of his subsequent walk homewards. What fearful shapes and shadows beset his path, amidst the dim and ghostly glare of a snowy night! With what wistful look did he eye every trembling ray of light streaming across the waste fields from some distant window! How often was he appalled by some shrub covered with snow, which like sheeted spectre beset his very path! How often did he shrink with curdling awe at the sound of his own steps on the frosty crust beneath his feet; and dread to look over his shoulder, lest he should behold some uncouth being tramping close behind him! and how often was he thrown into complete dismay by some rushing blast, howling among the trees, in the idea that it was the galloping Hessian on one of his nightly scourings.

---

1   *in linked … drawn out*   See John Milton's "L'Allegro" (1645), line 140.

All these, however, were mere terrors of the night, phantoms of the mind, that walk in darkness; and though he had seen many spectres in his time, and been more than once beset by Satan in diverse shapes, in his lonely perambulations, yet daylight put an end to all these evils; and he would have passed a pleasant life of it, in despite of the Devil and all his works, if his path had not been crossed by a being that causes more perplexity to mortal man, than ghosts, goblins, and the whole race of witches put together, and that was—a woman.

Among the musical disciples who assembled, one evening in each week, to receive his instructions in psalmody, was Katrina Van Tassel, the daughter and only child of a substantial Dutch farmer. She was a blooming lass of fresh eighteen; plump as a partridge; ripe and melting and rosy-cheeked as one of her father's peaches, and universally famed, not merely for her beauty, but her vast expectations. She was withal a little of a coquette, as might be perceived even in her dress, which was a mixture of ancient and modern fashions, as most suited to set off her charms. She wore the ornaments of pure yellow gold, which her great-great-grandmother had brought over from Saardam; the tempting stomacher[1] of the olden time, and withal a provokingly short petticoat, to display the prettiest foot and ankle in the country round.

Ichabod Crane had a soft and foolish heart toward the sex; and it is not to be wondered at, that so tempting a morsel soon found favour in his eyes, more especially after he had visited her in her paternal mansion. Old Baltus Van Tassel was a perfect picture of a thriving, contented, liberal-hearted farmer. He seldom, it is true, sent either his eyes or his thoughts beyond the boundaries of his own farm; but within those everything was snug, happy, and well-conditioned. He was satisfied with his wealth, but not proud of it, and piqued himself upon the hearty abundance, rather than the style in which he lived. His strong hold was situated on the banks of the Hudson, in one of those green, sheltered, fertile nooks, into which the Dutch farmers are so fond of nestling. A great elm tree spread its broad branches over it, at the foot of which bubbled up a spring of the softest and sweetest water, in a little kind of well, formed of a barrel, and then stole spar-

---

1   *Saardam*   Zaandam, city just north of Amsterdam;   *stomacher*   Ornamental panel worn in the opening of the bodice, fashionable until the mid- to late eighteenth century.

kling away through the grass, to a neighbouring brook, that babbled along among alders and dwarf willows. Hard by the farmhouse was a vast barn, that might have served for a church; every window and crevice of which seemed bursting forth with the treasures of the farm; the flail was busily resounding within it; swallows and martins skimmed twittering about the eaves, and rows of pigeons, some with one eye turned up, as if watching the weather, some with their heads under their wings, or buried in their bosoms, and others, swelling, and cooing, and bowing about their dames, were enjoying the sunshine on the roof. Sleek unwieldy porkers were grunting in the repose and abundance of their pens, from whence sallied forth, now and then, troops of sucking pigs, as if to snuff the air. A stately squadron of snowy geese were riding in an adjoining pond, convoying whole fleets of ducks; regiments of turkeys were gobbling about the farm yard, and guinea fowls fretting like ill-tempered housewives, with their peevish discontented cry. Before the barn door strutted the gallant cock, that pattern of a husband, a warrior, and a fine gentleman, clapping his burnished wings, and crowing in the pride and gladness of his heart—sometimes tearing up the earth with his feet, and then generously calling his ever-hungry family of wives and children to enjoy the rich morsel he had discovered.

The pedagogue's mouth watered, as he looked upon this sumptuous promise of luxurious winter fare. In his devouring mind's eye, he pictured to himself every roasting pig running about with a pudding in its belly,[1] and an apple in its mouth; the pigeons were snugly put to bed in a comfortable pie, and tucked in with a coverlet of crust; the geese were swimming in their own gravy; and the ducks pairing cosily in dishes, like snug married couples, with a decent competency of onion sauce; in the porkers he saw carved out the future sleek side of bacon, and juicy relishing ham; not a turkey, but he beheld daintily trussed up, with its gizzard under its wing, and, peradventure, a necklace of savoury sausages; and even bright chanticleer himself lay sprawling on his back, in a side dish, with uplifted claws, as if craving that quarter,[2] which his chivalrous spirit disdained to ask while living.

---

1   *roasting pig ... in its belly*   See Shakespeare's *1 Henry IV* 2.4.468–69: "that roasted Manningtree ox with the pudding in his belly."
2   *chanticleer*   Rooster;   *quarter*   Mercy.

As the enraptured Ichabod fancied all this, and as he rolled his great green eyes over the fat meadow lands, the rich fields of wheat, of rye, of buckwheat, and Indian corn, and the orchards burdened with ruddy fruit, which surrounded the warm tenement of Van Tassel, his heart yearned after the damsel who was to inherit these domains, and his imagination expanded with the idea, how they might be readily turned into cash, and the money invested in immense tracts of wild land, and shingle palaces in the wilderness. Nay, his busy fancy already put him in possession of his hopes, and presented to him the blooming Katrina, with a whole family of children, mounted on the top of a wagon loaded with household trumpery, with pots and kettles dangling beneath; and he beheld himself bestriding a pacing mare, with a colt at her heels, setting out for Kentucky, Tennessee, or the Lord knows where!

When he entered the house, the conquest of his heart was complete. It was one of those spacious farm-houses, with high-ridged, but lowly sloping roofs, built in the style handed down from the first Dutch settlers. The low, projecting eaves formed a piazza along the front, capable of being closed up in bad weather. Under this were hung flails, harness, various utensils of husbandry, and nets for fishing in the neighbouring river. Benches were built along the sides for summer use; and a great spinning wheel at one end, and a churn at the other, showed the various uses to which this important porch might be devoted. From this piazza the wondering Ichabod entered the hall, which formed the centre of the mansion, and the place of usual residence. Here rows of resplendent pewter, ranged on a long dresser, dazzled his eyes. In one corner stood a huge bag of wool ready to be spun; in another a quantity of linsey-woolsey[1] just from the loom; ears of Indian corn, and strings of dried apples and peaches, hung in gay festoons along the walls, mingled with the gaud of red peppers; and a door left ajar, gave him a peep into the best parlour, where the claw-footed chairs, and dark mahogany tables, shone like mirrors; andirons,[2] with their accompanying shovel and tongs, glistened from their covert of asparagus tops; mock oranges and conch shells decorated the mantlepiece; strings of various coloured birds'

---

1 *linsey-woolsey* Coarse fabric woven of both wool and linen threads.
2 *andirons* Iron supports for holding wood in a fireplace.

eggs were suspended above it; a great ostrich egg was hung from the centre of the room, and a corner cupboard, knowingly left open, displayed immense treasures of old silver and well-mended china.

From the moment Ichabod laid his eyes upon these regions of delight, the peace of his mind was at an end, and his only study was how to gain the affections of the peerless daughter of Van Tassel. In this enterprise, however, he had more real difficulties than generally fell to the lot of a knight-errant of yore, who seldom had anything but giants, enchanters, fiery dragons, and such like easily conquered adversaries, to contend with; and had to make his way merely through gates of iron and brass, and walls of adamant,[1] to the castle keep, where the lady of his heart was confined; all which he achieved as easily as a man would carve his way to the centre of a Christmas pie, and then the lady gave him her hand as a matter of course. Ichabod, on the contrary, had to win his way to the heart of a country coquette, beset with a labyrinth of whims and caprices, which were forever presenting new difficulties and impediments, and he had to encounter a host of fearful adversaries of real flesh and blood, the numerous rustic admirers, who beset every portal to her heart, keeping a watchful and angry eye upon each other, but ready to fly out in the common cause against any new competitor.

Among these, the most formidable was a burly, roaring, roistering blade, of the name of Abraham, or, according to the Dutch abbreviation, Brom Van Brunt, the hero of the country round, which rung with his feats of strength and hardihood. He was broad shouldered and double jointed, with short curly black hair, and a bluff, but not unpleasant countenance, having a mingled air of fun and arrogance. From his Herculean frame and great powers of limb, he had received the nickname of Brom Bones, by which he was universally known. He was famed for great knowledge and skill in horsemanship, being as dexterous on horseback as a Tartar.[2] He was foremost at all races and cock-fights, and with the ascendancy which bodily strength always acquires in rustic life, was the umpire in all disputes, setting his hat on one side, and giving his decisions with an air and tone admitting of no gainsay or appeal. He was always ready for either a fight or a

---

1   *adamant*   Hard rock or mineral, often diamond.
2   *Tartar*   Person from the central Asian area formerly known as Tartary.

frolic; had more mischief than ill-will in his composition; and with all his overbearing roughness, there was a strong dash of waggish good humour at bottom. He had three or four boon companions of his own stamp, who regarded him as their model, and at the head of whom he scoured the country, attending every scene of feud or merriment for miles around. In cold weather he was distinguished by a fur cap, surmounted with a flaunting fox's tail, and when the folks at a country gathering descried this well-known crest at a distance, whisking about among a squad of hard riders, they always stood by for a squall. Sometimes his crew would be heard dashing along past the farm-houses at midnight with whoop and halloo, like a troop of Don Cossacks,[1] and the old dames, startled out of their sleep, would listen for a moment till the hurry-scurry had clattered by, and then exclaim, "Ay, there goes Brom Bones and his gang!" The neighbours looked upon him with a mixture of awe, admiration, and good-will; and when any mad-cap prank, or rustic brawl, occurred in the vicinity, always shook their heads, and warranted Brom Bones was at the bottom of it.

This rantipole hero had for some time singled out the blooming Katrina for the object of his uncouth gallantries, and though his amorous toyings were something like the gentle caresses and endearments of a bear, yet it was whispered that she did not altogether discourage his hopes. Certain it is, his advances were signals for rival candidates to retire, who felt no inclination to cross a line in his amours; insomuch, that when his horse was seen tied to Van Tassel's paling, on a Sunday night (a sure sign that his master was courting, or, as it is termed, "sparking," within), all other suitors passed by in despair, and carried the war into other quarters.

Such was the formidable rival with whom Ichabod Crane had to contend, and, considering all things, a stouter man than he would have shrunk from the competition, and a wiser man would have despaired. He had, however, a happy mixture of pliability and perseverance in his nature; he was in form and spirit like a supple jack[2]—yielding, but tough; though he bent, he never broke; and though he bowed beneath the slightest pressure, yet, the moment it was away—jerk!—he was as erect, and carried his head as high as ever.

---

1   *Don Cossacks*   Self-governing, military people who inhabited areas around the Don River in Russia.
2   *jack*   Wood of the jackfruit tree.

To have taken the field openly against his rival, would have been madness; for he was not man to be thwarted in his amours, any more than that stormy lover, Achilles.[1] Ichabod, therefore, made his advances in a quiet and gently-insinuating manner. Under cover of his character of singing master, he made frequent visits at the farmhouse; not that he had anything to apprehend from the meddlesome interference of parents, which is so often a stumbling block in the path of lovers. Balt Van Tassel was an easy, indulgent soul; he loved his daughter better even than his pipe, and like a reasonable man, and an excellent father, let her have her way in everything. His notable little wife too, had enough to do to attend to her housekeeping and manage the poultry, for, as she sagely observed, ducks and geese are foolish things, and must be looked after, but girls can take care of themselves. Thus while the busy dame bustled about the house, or plied her spinning wheel at one end of the piazza, honest Balt would sit smoking his evening pipe at the other, watching the achievements of a little wooden warrior, who, armed with a sword in each hand, was most valiantly fighting the wind on the pinnacle of the barn. In the mean time, Ichabod would carry on his suit with the daughter by the side of the spring under the great elm, or sauntering along in the twilight, that hour so favourable to the lover's eloquence.

I profess not to know how women's hearts are wooed and won. To me they have always been matters of riddle and admiration. Some seem to have but one vulnerable point, or door of access; while others have a thousand avenues, and may be captured in a thousand different ways. It is a great triumph of skill to gain the former, but a still greater proof of generalship to maintain possession of the latter, for the man must battle for his fortress at every door and window. He that wins a thousand common hearts, is therefore entitled to some renown; but he who keeps undisputed sway over the heart of a coquette, is indeed a hero. Certain it is, this was not the case with the redoubtable Brom Bones; and from the moment Ichabod Crane made his advances, the interests of the former evidently declined; his horse was no longer seen tied at the palings on Sunday nights, and a deadly feud gradually arose between him and the preceptor of Sleepy Hollow.

---

1   *Achilles*   Protagonist of Homer's *Iliad*, who is made bitterly disappointed by the loss of his enslaved concubine Briseis; Achilles is also known for his intense affection for fellow-warrior Patroclus.

Brom, who had a degree of rough chivalry in his nature, would fain have carried matters to open warfare, and settled their pretensions to the lady, according to the mode of those most concise and simple reasoners, the knights-errant of yore—by single combat; but Ichabod was too conscious of the superior might of his adversary to enter the lists against him; he had overheard the boast of Bones, that he would "double the schoolmaster up, and put him on a shelf"; and he was too wary to give him an opportunity. There was something extremely provoking in this obstinately pacific system; it left Brom no alternative but to draw upon the funds of rustic waggery in his disposition, and play off boorish practical jokes upon his rival. Ichabod became the object of whimsical persecution to Bones, and his gang of rough riders. They harried his hitherto peaceful domains; smoked out his singing school, by stopping up the chimney; broke into the schoolhouse at night, in spite of its formidable fastenings of withe and window stakes, and turned every thing topsy-turvy, so that the poor schoolmaster began to think all the witches in the country held their meetings there. But what was still more annoying, Brom took all opportunities of turning him into ridicule in presence of his mistress, and had a scoundrel dog, whom he taught to whine in the most ludicrous manner, and introduced as a rival of Ichabod's, to instruct her in psalmody.

In this way, matters went on for some time, without producing any material effect on the relative situation of the contending powers. On a fine autumnal afternoon, Ichabod, in pensive mood, sat enthroned on the lofty stool whence he usually watched all the concerns of his little literary realm. In his hand he swayed a ferule,[1] that sceptre of despotic power; the birch of justice reposed on three nails, behind the throne, a constant terror to evil doers; while on the desk before him might be seen sundry contraband articles and prohibited weapons, detected upon the persons of idle urchins, such as half-munched apples, popguns, whirligigs,[2] fly-cages, and whole legions of rampant little paper game cocks. Apparently there had been some appalling act of justice recently inflicted, for his scholars were all busily intent upon their books, or slyly whispering behind them with one eye kept upon

---

1 *ferule* Rod for corporal punishment.
2 *whirligigs* Spinning tops.

the master; and a kind of buzzing stillness reigned throughout the schoolroom. It was suddenly interrupted by the appearance of a negro in tow-cloth jacket and trousers, a round crowned fragment of a hat, like the cap of Mercury,[1] and mounted on the back of a ragged, wild, half-broken colt, which he managed with a rope by way of halter. He came clattering up to the school door with an invitation to Ichabod to attend a merry-making, or "quilting frolick," to be held that evening at Mynheer[2] Van Tassel's, and having delivered his message with that air of importance, and effort at fine language, which a negro is apt to display on petty embassies of the kind, he dashed over the brook, and was seen scampering away up the hollow, full of the importance and hurry of his mission.

All was now bustle and hubbub in the late quiet school room. The scholars were hurried through their lessons, without stopping at trifles; those who were nimble, skipped over half with impunity, and those who were tardy, had a smart application now and then in the rear, to quicken their speed, or help them over a tall word. Books were flung aside, without being put away on the shelves; inkstands were overturned, benches thrown down, and the whole school turned loose an hour before the usual time; bursting forth like a legion of young imps, yelping and racketing about the green, in joy at their early emancipation.

The gallant Ichabod now spent at least an extra half hour at his toilet,[3] brushing and furbishing up his best, and indeed only suit of rusty black, and arranging his looks by a bit of broken looking glass, that hung up in the school house. That he might make his appearance before his mistress in the true style of a cavalier, he borrowed a horse from the farmer with whom he was domiciliated, a choleric old Dutchman, of the name of Hans Van Ripper, and thus gallantly mounted, issued forth like a knight-errant in quest of adventures. But it is meet I should, in the true spirit of romantic story, give some account of the looks and equipments of my hero and his steed. The animal he bestrode was a broken-down plough horse, that had

---

1   *tow-cloth*   Coarse fabric woven from the shorter fibers of the flax plant, often worn by the very poor or by enslaved people (slavery was not abolished in New York until 1827); *cap of Mercury* Winged helmet worn by Mercury, the messenger god in Roman mythology.

2   *Mynheer*   Polite form of address for a Dutchman.

3   *toilet*   I.e., dressing table, where one would groom oneself.

outlived almost everything but his viciousness. He was gaunt and shagged, with a ewe neck and hammer head; his rusty mane and tail were tangled and knotted with burrs; one eye had lost its pupil, and was glaring and spectral, but the other had the gleam of a genuine devil in it. Still he must have had fire and mettle in his day, if we may judge from his name, which was Gunpowder. He had, in fact, been a favourite steed of his master's, the choleric Van Ripper, who was a furious rider, and had infused, very probably, some of his own spirit into the animal, for, old and broken-down as he looked, there was more lurking deviltry in him than in any young filly in the country.

Ichabod was a suitable figure for such a steed. He rode with short stirrups, which brought his knees nearly up to the pommel of the saddle; his sharp elbows stuck out like grasshoppers'; he carried his whip perpendicularly in his hand, like a sceptre, and as the horse jogged on, the motion of his arms was not unlike the flapping of a pair of wings. A small wool hat rested on the top of his nose, for so his scanty strip of forehead might be called, and the skirts of his black coat fluttered out almost to the horse's tail. Such was the appearance of Ichabod and his steed, as they shambled out of the gate of Hans Van Ripper, and it was altogether such an apparition as is seldom to be met with in broad daylight.

It was, as I have said, a fine autumnal day, the sky was clear and serene, and nature wore that rich and golden livery which we always associate with the idea of abundance. The forests had put on their sober brown and yellow, while some trees of the tenderer kind had been nipped by the frosts into brilliant dyes of orange, purple, and scarlet. Streaming files of wild ducks began to make their appearance high in the air; the bark of the squirrel might be heard from the groves of beech and hickory nuts, and the pensive whistle of the quail at intervals from the neighbouring stubble field.

The small birds were taking their farewell banquets. In the fullness of their revelry, they fluttered, chirping and frolicking, from bush to bush, and tree to tree, capricious from the very profusion and variety around them. There was the honest cock-robin,[1] the favourite game of stripling sportsmen, with its loud querulous note; and the twittering

---

1   *cock-robin*   I.e., male robin.

blackbirds flying in sable clouds; and the golden winged woodpecker, with his crimson crest, his broad black gorget,[1] and splendid plumage; and the cedar bird, with its red tipped wings and yellow tipped tail, and its little monteiro cap[2] of feathers; and the blue jay, that noisy coxcomb, in his gay light blue coat and white under clothes, screaming and chattering, nodding, and bobbing, and bowing, and pretending to be on good terms with every songster of the grove.

As Ichabod jogged slowly on his way, his eye, ever open to every symptom of culinary abundance, ranged with delight over the treasures of jolly autumn. On all sides he beheld vast store of apples, some hanging in oppressive opulence on the trees, some gathered into baskets and barrels for the market, others heaped up in rich piles for the cider-press. Further on he beheld great fields of Indian corn, with its golden ears peeping from their leafy coverts, and holding out the promise of cakes and hasty pudding; and the yellow pumpkins lying beneath them, turning up their fair round bellies to the sun, and giving ample prospects of the most luxurious of pies; and anon he passed the fragrant buckwheat fields, breathing the odour of the beehive, and as he beheld them, soft anticipations stole over his mind of dainty slap-jacks, well buttered, and garnished with honey or treacle, by the delicate little dimpled hand of Katrina Van Tassel.

Thus feeding his mind with many sweet thoughts and "sugared suppositions," he journeyed along the sides of a range of hills which look out upon some of the goodliest scenes of the mighty Hudson. The sun gradually wheeled his broad disk down into the west. The wide bosom of the Tappaan Zee lay motionless and glassy, excepting that here and there a gentle undulation waved and prolonged the blue shadow of the distant mountain: a few amber clouds floated in the sky, without a breath of air to move them. The horizon was of a fine golden tint, changing gradually into a pure apple green, and from that into a deep blue of the mid-heaven. A slanting ray lingered on the woody crests of the precipices that overhung some parts of the river, giving greater depth to the dark grey and purple of their rocky sides. A sloop was loitering in the distance, dropping slowly down with the tide, her sail hanging uselessly against the mast, and as the

1 *gorget* Throat.
2 *the cedar bird* The cedar waxwing; *monteiro cap* Spanish hunting cap.

reflection of the sky gleamed along the still water, it seemed as if the vessel was suspended in the air.

It was toward evening that Ichabod arrived at the castle of the Heer Van Tassel, which he found thronged with the pride and flower of the adjacent country. Old farmers, a spare, leathern-faced race, in homespun coats and small clothes,[1] blue stockings, huge shoes and magnificent pewter buckles. Their brisk withered little dames in close crimped caps, long waisted short gowns, homespun petticoats, with scissors and pincushions, and gay calico pockets, hanging on the outside. Buxom lasses, almost as antiquated as their mothers, excepting where a straw hat, a fine ribbon, or perhaps a white frock, gave symptoms of city innovations. The sons, in short square-skirted coats with rows of stupendous brass buttons, and their hair generally queued[2] in the fashion of the times, especially if they could procure an eel-skin for the purpose, it being esteemed throughout the country as a potent nourisher and strengthener of the hair.

Brom Bones, however, was the hero of the scene, having come to the gathering on his favourite steed Daredevil, a creature, like himself, full of mettle and mischief, and which no one but himself could manage. He was in fact noted for preferring vicious animals, given to all kinds of tricks, which kept the rider in constant risk of his neck, and held a tractable well-broken horse as unworthy a lad of spirit.

Fain would I pause to dwell upon the world of charms that burst upon the enraptured gaze of my hero, as he entered the state parlour of Van Tassel's mansion. Not those of the bevy of buxom lasses, with their luxurious display of red and white: but the ample charms of a genuine Dutch country tea-table, in the sumptuous time of autumn. Such heaped up platters of cakes of various and almost indescribable kinds, known only to experienced Dutch housewives. There was the doughty dough-nut, the tenderer oly koek,[3] and the crisp and crumbling cruller; sweet cakes and short cakes, ginger cakes and honey cakes, and the whole family of cakes. And then there were apple pies and peach pies and pumpkin pies; not to mention slices of ham and smoked beef, together with broiled shad and roasted chickens; besides delectable dishes of preserved plums, and peaches, and pears, and

---

1 *small clothes* Breeches; trousers.
2 *queued* Worn in a braid or low ponytail down the back of the head.
3 *oly koek* Dutch donut.

quinces; with bowls of milk and cream, all mingled higgledy-piggledy, pretty much as I have enumerated them, with the motherly tea-pot sending up its clouds of vapour from the midst—Heaven bless the mark! I want breath and time to discuss this banquet as it deserves, and am too eager to get on with my story. Happily, Ichabod Crane was not in so great a hurry as his historian, but did ample justice to every dainty.

He was a kind and thankful toad, whose heart dilated in proportion as his skin was filled with good cheer, and whose spirits rose with eating, as some men's do with drink. He could not help, too, rolling his large eyes round him as he ate, and chuckling with the possibility that he might one day be lord of all this scene of almost unimaginable luxury and splendour. Then, he thought, how soon he'd turn his back upon the old schoolhouse; snap his fingers in the face of Hans Van Ripper, and every other niggardly patron, and kick any itinerant pedagogue out of doors that dared to call him comrade!

Old Baltus Van Tassel moved about among his guests with a face dilated with content and good humour, round and jolly as the harvest moon. His hospitable attentions were brief, but expressive, being confined to a shake of the hand, a slap on the shoulder, a loud laugh, and a pressing invitation to "reach to, and help themselves."

And now the sound of the music from the common room or hall, summoned to the dance. The musician was an old grey-headed negro, who had been the itinerant orchestra of the neighbourhood for more than half a century. His instrument was as old and battered as himself. The greater part of the time he scraped on two or three strings, accompanying every movement of the bow with a motion of the head; bowing almost to the ground, and stamping with his foot whenever a fresh couple were to start.

Ichabod prided himself upon his dancing as much as upon his vocal powers. Not a limb, not a fibre about him was idle, and to have seen his loosely hung frame in full motion, and clattering about the room, you would have thought Saint Vitus[1] himself, that blessed patron of the dance, was figuring before you in person. He was the admiration of all the negroes, who, having gathered, of all ages and

---

1   *Saint Vitus* Patron saint of dancers—as well as of epileptics. The name "Saint Vitus's Dance" was given to the condition now known as Sydenham's chorea, which causes uncontrollable jerking movements.

sizes, from the farm and the neighbourhood, stood forming a pyramid of shining black faces at every door and window, gazing with delight at the scene, rolling their white eyeballs, and showing grinning rows of ivory from ear to ear. How could the flogger of urchins be otherwise than animated and joyous; the lady of his heart was his partner in the dance; and smiled graciously in reply to all his amorous oglings, while Brom Bones, sorely smitten with love and jealousy, sat brooding by himself in one corner.

When the dance was at an end, Ichabod was attracted to a knot of the sager folks, who, with old Van Tassel, sat smoking at one end of the piazza, gossiping over former times and drawing out long stories about the war.

This neighbourhood, at the time of which I am speaking, was one of those highly favoured places which abound with chronicle and great men. The British and American line had run near it during the war; it had, therefore, been the scene of marauding, and been infested with refugees, cow boys,[1] and all kinds of border chivalry. Just sufficient time had elapsed to enable each story teller to dress up his tale with a little becoming fiction, and in the indistinctness of his recollection, to make himself the hero of every exploit.

There was the story of Doffue Martling, a large, blue-bearded Dutchman, who had nearly taken a British frigate with an old iron nine-pounder from a mud breastwork,[2] only that his gun burst at the sixth discharge. And there was an old gentleman who shall be nameless, being too rich a mynheer to be lightly mentioned, who in the battle of Whiteplains, being an excellent master of defence, parried a musket ball with a small sword, insomuch that he absolutely felt it whiz round the blade, and glance off at the hilt: in proof of which, he was ready at any time to show the sword, with the hilt a little bent. There were several more who had been equally great in the field, not one of whom but was persuaded that he had a considerable hand in bringing the war to a happy termination.

But all these were nothing to the tales of ghosts and apparitions that succeeded. The neighbourhood is rich in legendary treasures of

---

1   *cow boys*   British loyalists in New York who conducted brutal raids during the Revolutionary War.

2   *nine-pounder*   Gun or cannon that fires nine-pound balls;   *breastwork*   Rough, temporary fortification.

the kind. Local tales and superstitions thrive best in these sheltered, long settled retreats; but they are trampled under foot, by the shifting throng that forms the population of most of our country places. Besides, there is no encouragement for ghosts in the generality of our villages, for they have scarce had time to take their first nap, and turn themselves in their graves, before their surviving friends have travelled away from the neighbourhood, so that when they turn out of a night to walk the rounds, they have no acquaintance left to call upon. This is perhaps the reason why we so seldom hear of ghosts excepting in our long-established Dutch communities.

The immediate cause, however, of the prevalence of supernatural stories in these parts, was doubtless owing to the vicinity of Sleepy Hollow. There was a contagion in the very air that blew from that haunted region; it breathed forth an atmosphere of dreams and fancies infecting all the land. Several of the Sleepy Hollow people were present at Van Tassel's, and, as usual, were doling out their wild and wonderful legends. Many dismal tales were told about funeral trains, and mournful cries and wailings heard and seen about the great tree where the unfortunate Major André[1] was taken, and which stood in the neighbourhood. Some mention was made also of the woman in white, that haunted the dark glen at Raven Rock, and was often heard to shriek on winter nights before a storm, having perished there in the snow. The chief part of the stories, however, turned upon the favourite spectre of Sleepy Hollow, the headless horseman, who had been heard several times of late, patrolling the country; and it was said, tethered his horse nightly among the graves in the churchyard.

The sequestered situation of this church seems always to have made it a favourite haunt of troubled spirits. It stands on a knoll, surrounded by locust trees and lofty elms, from among which its decent, whitewashed walls shine modestly forth, like Christian purity, beaming through the shades of retirement. A gentle slope descends from it to a silver sheet of water, bordered by high trees, between which, peeps may be caught at the blue hills of the Hudson. To look upon its grass-grown yard, where the sunbeams seem to sleep so quietly, one would think that here at least the dead might rest in peace. On

---

1 *Major André* John André (1751–80), British officer who was hanged for being a spy and for helping the American officer Benedict Arnold betray his army.

one side of the church extends a wide woody dell, along which raves a large brook among broken rocks and trunks of fallen trees. Over a deep black part of the stream, not far from the church, was formerly thrown a wooden bridge; the road that led to it, and the bridge itself, were thickly shaded by overhanging trees, which cast a gloom about it, even in the daytime; but occasioned a fearful darkness at night. Such was one of the favourite haunts of the headless horseman, and the place where he was most frequently encountered. The tale was told of old Brouwer, a most heretical disbeliever in ghosts, that he met the horseman returning from his foray into Sleepy Hollow, and was obliged to get up behind him; that they galloped over bush and brake, over hill and swamp, until they reached the bridge, when the horseman suddenly turned into a skeleton, threw old Brouwer into the brook, and sprang away over the tree-tops with a clap of thunder.

This story was immediately matched by a thrice marvellous adventure of Brom Bones, who made light of the galloping Hessian as an errant jockey. He affirmed, that on returning one night from the neighbouring village of Sing-Sing, he had been overtaken by this midnight trooper; that he had offered to race with him for a bowl of punch, and would have won it too, for Daredevil beat the goblin horse all hollow, but just as they came to the church bridge, the Hessian bolted, and vanished in a flash of fire.

All these tales, told in that drowsy undertone with which men talk in the dark, the countenances of the listeners only now and then receiving a casual gleam from the glare of a pipe, sunk deep in the mind of Ichabod. He repaid them in kind with large extracts from his invaluable author, Cotton Mather, and added many marvellous events that had taken place in his native state of Connecticut, and fearful sights which he had seen in his nightly walks about Sleepy Hollow.

The revel now gradually broke up. The old farmers gathered together their families in their wagons, and were heard for some time rattling along the hollow roads, and over the distant hills. Some of the damsels, mounted on pillions behind their favourite swains, and their light-hearted laughter mingling with the clatter of hoofs, echoed along the silent woodlands, sounding fainter and fainter until they gradually died away—and the late scene of noise and frolic was all silent and deserted. Ichabod only lingered behind, according to the custom of country lovers, to have a tête-a-tête with the heiress; fully convinced that he was now on the high road to success. What passed at this interview I will not pretend to say, for in fact I do not know. Something, however, I fear me, must have gone wrong, for he certainly sallied forth, after no very great interval, with an air quite desolate and chopfallen—Oh these women! these women! Could that girl have been playing off any of her coquettish tricks? Was her encouragement of the poor pedagogue all a mere sham to secure her conquest of his rival? Heaven only knows, not I! Let it suffice to say, Ichabod stole forth with the air of one who had been sacking a hen roost, rather than a fair lady's heart. Without looking to the right or left to notice the scene of rural wealth, on which he had so often gloated, he went straight to the stable, and with several hearty cuffs and kicks, roused his steed most uncourteously from the comfortable quarters in which he was soundly sleeping, dreaming of mountains of corn and oats, and whole valleys of timothy and clover.

It was the very witching time of night[1] that Ichabod, heavy-hearted and bedrooped, pursued his travel homewards, along the sides of the lofty hills which rise above Tarry Town, and which he had traversed so cheerily in the afternoon. The hour was as dismal as himself. Far below him the Tappaan Zee spread its dusky and indistinct waste of waters, with here and there the tall mast of a sloop, riding quietly at anchor under the land. In the dead hush of midnight, he could even hear the barking of the watch-dog from the opposite shore of the Hudson; but it was so vague and faint as only to give an idea of his distance from this faithful companion of man. Now and then, too, the long-drawn crowing of a cock, accidentally awakened, would sound far, far off, from some farm house away among the hills—but it was like a dreaming sound in his ear. No signs of life occurred near him, but occasionally the melancholy chirp of a cricket, or perhaps the guttural twang of a bull frog, from a neighbouring marsh, as if sleeping uncomfortably, and turning suddenly in his bed.

All the stories of ghosts and goblins that Ichabod had heard in the afternoon, now came crowding upon his recollection. The night grew darker and darker; the stars seemed to sink deeper in the sky, and driving clouds occasionally hid them from his sight. He had never felt

---

1   *It was ... of night*   See Shakespeare's *Hamlet* 3.2.419.

so lonely and dismal. He was, moreover, approaching the very place where many of the scenes of the ghost stories had been laid. In the centre of the road stood an enormous tulip tree, which towered like a giant above all the other trees of the neighbourhood, and formed a kind of land-mark. Its limbs were vast, gnarled, and fantastic, twisting down almost to the earth, and rising again into the air, and they would have formed trunks for ordinary trees. It was connected with the tragical story of the unfortunate André, who had been taken prisoner hard by it, and it was universally known by the name of Major André's tree. The common people regarded it with a mixture of respect and superstition, partly out of sympathy for the memory of its ill-starred namesake, and partly from the tales, strange sights, and doleful lamentations, told concerning it.

As Ichabod approached this fearful tree, he began to whistle; he thought his whistle was answered: it was but a blast sweeping sharply through the dry branches. As he approached a little nearer, he thought he saw something white, hanging in the midst of the tree: he paused and ceased whistling; but on looking more narrowly, perceived that it was a place where the tree had been scathed by lightning, and the white wood laid bare. Suddenly he heard a groan—his teeth chattered, and his knees smote against the saddle: it was but the rubbing of one huge bough upon another, as they were swayed about by the breeze. He passed the tree in safety, but new perils lay still before him.

About two hundred yards from the tree, a small brook crossed the road, and ran into a marshy and thickly wooded glen, known by the name of Wiley's Swamp. A few rough logs, laid side by side, served for a bridge over this stream. On that side of the road where the brook entered the wood, a group of oaks and chestnuts, matted thick with wild grape vines, threw a cavernous gloom over it. To pass this bridge, was the severest trial. It was at this identical spot that the unfortunate André was captured, and under the covert of those chestnuts and vines were the sturdy yeomen concealed who surprised him. This has ever since been considered a haunted stream, and fearful are the feelings of the schoolboy who has to pass it alone after dark.

As he approached the stream, his heart began to thump; he, however, summoned up all his resolution, gave his horse half a score of kicks in the ribs, and attempted to dash briskly across the bridge; but instead of starting forward, the perverse old animal made a lateral movement, and ran broadside against the fence. Ichabod, whose fears increased with the delay, jerked the reins on the other side, and kicked lustily with the contrary foot: it was all in vain; his steed started, it is true, but it was only to plunge to the opposite side of the road into a thicket of brambles and alder bushes. The schoolmaster now bestowed both whip and heel upon the starveling ribs of old Gunpowder, who dashed forward, snuffing and snorting, but came to a stand just by the bridge with a suddenness that had nearly sent his rider sprawling over his head. Just at this moment a plashy tramp by the side of the bridge caught the sensitive ear of Ichabod. In the dark shadow of the grove, on the margin of the brook, he beheld something huge, misshapen, black and towering. It stirred not, but seemed gathered up in the gloom, like some gigantic monster ready to spring upon the traveller.

The hair of the affrighted pedagogue rose upon his head with terror. What was to be done? To turn and fly was now too late; and besides, what chance was there of escaping ghost or goblin, if such it was, which can ride upon the wings of the wind? Summoning up, therefore, a show of courage, he demanded in stammering accents, "Who are you?" He received no reply. He repeated his demand in a still more agitated voice. Still there was no answer. Once more he cudgelled the sides of the inflexible Gunpowder, and shutting his eyes, broke forth with involuntary fervour into a psalm tune. Just then the shadowy object of alarm put itself in motion, and with a scramble and a bound, stood at once in the middle of the road. Though the night was dark and dismal, yet the form of the unknown might now in some degree be ascertained. He appeared to be a horseman of large dimensions, and mounted on a black horse of powerful frame. He made no offer of molestation or sociability, but kept aloof on one side of the road, jogging along on the blind side of old Gunpowder, who had now got over his fright and waywardness.

Ichabod, who had no relish for this strange midnight companion, and bethought himself of the adventure of Brom Bones with the galloping Hessian, now quickened his steed, in hopes of leaving him behind. The stranger, however, quickened his horse to an equal pace; Ichabod pulled up, and fell into a walk, thinking to lag behind—the other did the same. His heart began to sink within him; he endeavoured to resume his psalm tune, but his parched tongue clove to the roof of his mouth, and he could not utter a stave.[1] There was something in the moody and dogged silence of this pertinacious companion, that was mysterious and appalling. It was soon fearfully accounted for. On mounting a rising ground, which brought the figure of his fellow traveller in relief against the sky, gigantic in height, and muffled in a cloak, Ichabod was horror-struck, on perceiving that he was headless! but his horror was still more increased, on observing, that the head, which should have rested on his shoulders, was carried before him on the pommel of the saddle! His terror rose to desperation; he rained a shower of kicks and blows upon Gunpowder, hoping, by a sudden movement, to give his companion the slip—but the spectre started full jump with him. Away, then, they dashed, through thick and thin; stones flying, and sparks flashing, at every bound. Ichabod's flimsy garments fluttered in the air, as he stretched his long lank body away over his horse's head, in the eagerness of his flight.

They had now reached the road which turns off to Sleepy Hollow; but Gunpowder, who seemed possessed with a demon, instead of keeping up it, made an opposite turn, and plunged headlong down hill to the left. This road leads through a sandy hollow shaded by trees for about a quarter of a mile, where it crosses the bridge famous in goblin story, and just beyond swells the green knoll on which stands the whitewashed church.

As yet the panic of the steed had given his unskilful rider an apparent advantage in the chase, but just as he had got half way through the hollow, the girths of the saddle gave way, and he felt it slipping from under him; he seized it by the pommel, and endeavoured to hold it firm, but in vain; and had just time to save himself by clasping old Gunpowder round the neck, when the saddle fell to the earth, and he heard it trampled under foot by his pursuer. For a moment the terror of Hans Van Ripper's wrath passed across his mind—for it was his Sunday saddle; but this was no time for petty fears: the goblin was hard on his haunches; and, unskilful rider that he was! he had much ado to maintain his seat; sometimes slipping on one side, sometimes on another, and sometimes jolted on the high ridge of his horse's back bone, with a violence that he verily feared would cleave him asunder.

---

1 *stave* Verse.

An opening in the trees now cheered him with the hopes that the Church Bridge was at hand. The wavering reflection of a silver star in the bosom of the brook told him that he was not mistaken. He saw the walls of the church dimly glaring under the trees beyond. He recollected the place where Brom Bones' ghostly competitor had disappeared. "If I can but reach that bridge," thought Ichabod, "I am safe."[1] Just then he heard the black steed panting and blowing close behind him; he fancied he felt his hot breath. Another convulsive kick in the ribs, and old Gunpowder sprung upon the bridge; he thundered over the resounding planks; he gained the opposite side, and now Ichabod cast a look behind to see if his pursuer should vanish, according to rule, in a flash of fire and brimstone. Just then he saw the goblin rising in his stirrups, and in the very act of hurling his head at him. Ichabod endeavoured to dodge the horrible missile, but too late. It encountered his cranium with a tremendous crash—he was tumbled headlong into the dust, and Gunpowder, the black steed, and the goblin rider, passed by like a whirlwind.

The next morning the old horse was found without his saddle, and the bridle under his feet, soberly cropping the grass at his master's gate. Ichabod did not make his appearance at breakfast—dinner-hour came, but no Ichabod. The boys assembled at the schoolhouse, and strolled idly about the banks of the brook; but no schoolmaster. Hans Van Ripper now began to feel some uneasiness about the fate of poor Ichabod, and his saddle. An inquiry was set on foot, and after diligent investigation they came upon his traces. In one part of the road leading to the church, was found the saddle trampled in the dirt; the tracks of horses' hoofs, deeply dented in the road, and evidently at furious speed, were traced to the bridge, beyond which, on the bank of a broad part of the brook, where the water ran deep and black, was found the hat of the unfortunate Ichabod, and close beside it a shattered pumpkin.

The brook was searched, but the body of the schoolmaster was not to be discovered. Hans Van Ripper, as executor of his estate, examined the bundle which contained all his worldly effects. They consisted of two old shirts and a half; two stocks for the neck;[2] a

---

1 *If I can … I am safe* Crane hopes to cross the river, holding to the common superstition that ghosts and supernatural beings were unable to cross bodies of running water.
2 *stocks for the neck* Neckties.

pair of worsted stockings with holes in them; an old pair of corduroy small-clothes; a book of psalm tunes full of dog's ears; a pitch pipe out of order; a rusty razor; a small pot of bear's grease for the hair, and a cast-iron comb. As to the books and furniture of the schoolhouse, they belonged to the community, excepting Cotton Mather's History of Witchcraft, a New England Almanac, and a book of dreams and fortune telling, in which last was a sheet of foolscap[1] much scribbled and blotted, by several fruitless attempts to make a copy of verses in honour of the heiress of Van Tassel. These magic books and the poetic scrawl were forthwith consigned to the flames by Hans Van Ripper, who from that time forward determined to send his children no more to school, observing, that he never knew any good come of this same reading and writing. Whatever money the schoolmaster possessed, and he had received his quarter's pay but a day or two before, he must have had about his person at the time of his disappearance.

The mysterious event caused much speculation at the Church on the following Sunday. Knots of gazers and gossips were collected in the churchyard, at the bridge, and at the spot where the hat and pumpkin had been found. The stories of Brouwer, of Bones, and a whole budget of others, were called to mind; and when they had diligently considered them all, and compared them with the symptoms of the present case, they shook their heads, and came to the conclusion, that Ichabod had been carried off by the galloping Hessian. As he was a bachelor, and in nobody's debt, nobody troubled his head any more about him, the school was removed to a different quarter of the hollow, and another pedagogue reigned in his stead.

It is true, an old farmer, who had been down to New York on a visit several years after, and from whom this account of the ghostly adventure was received, brought home the intelligence that Ichabod Crane was still alive; that he had left the neighbourhood partly through fear of the goblin and Hans Van Ripper, and partly in mortification at having been suddenly dismissed by the heiress; that he had changed his quarters to a distant part of the country; had kept school and studied law at the same time; had been admitted to the bar, turned politician, electioneered, written for the newspapers, and finally had

---

1 *foolscap*   Standard-sized writing paper.

been made a Justice of the Ten Pound Court.[1] Brom Bones too, who, shortly after his rival's disappearance, conducted the blooming Katrina in triumph to the altar, was observed to look exceedingly knowing whenever the story of Ichabod was related, and always burst into a hearty laugh at the mention of the pumpkin; which led some to suspect that he knew more about the matter than he chose to tell.

The old country wives, however, who are the best judges of these matters, maintain to this day, that Ichabod was spirited away by supernatural means; and it is a favourite story often told about the neighbourhood round the winter evening fire. The bridge became more than ever an object of superstitious awe, and that may be the reason why the road has been altered of late years, so as to approach the church by the border of the millpond. The schoolhouse being deserted, soon fell to decay, and was reported to be haunted by the ghost of the unfortunate pedagogue; and the plough boy, loitering homeward of a still summer evening, has often fancied his voice at a distance, chanting a melancholy psalm tune among the tranquil solitudes of Sleepy Hollow.

POSTSCRIPT,
FOUND IN THE HANDWRITING OF MR. KNICKER-BOCKER.

The preceding Tale is given, almost in the precise words in which I heard it related at a corporation meeting of the ancient city of the Manhattoes, at which were present many of its sagest and most illustrious burghers.[2] The narrator was a pleasant, shabby, gentlemanly old fellow, in pepper and salt clothes, with a sadly humorous face, and one whom I strongly suspected of being poor, he made such efforts to be entertaining. When his story was concluded, there was much laughter and approbation, particularly from two or three deputy aldermen, who had been asleep the greater part of the time. There was, however, one tall, dry-looking old gentleman, with beetling eyebrows, who maintained a grave and rather severe face throughout; now and then folding his arms, inclining his head, and looking down

---

1 *Ten Pound Court* Small-claims court (where only claims under the value of ten pounds were tried).

2 *burghers* Citizens.

upon the floor, as if turning a doubt over in his mind. He was one of your wary men, who never laugh but upon good grounds—when they have reason and the law on their side. When the mirth of the rest of the company had subsided, and silence was restored, he leaned one arm on the elbow of his chair, and sticking the other a-kimbo, demanded, with a slight, but exceedingly sage motion of the head, and contraction of the brow, what was the moral of the story, and what it went to prove.

The storyteller, who was just putting a glass of wine to his lips, as a refreshment after his toils, paused for a moment, looked at his inquirer with an air of infinite deference, and lowering the glass slowly to the table, observed, that the story was intended most logically to prove,

"That there is no situation in life but has its advantages and pleasures, provided we will but take a joke as we find it:

"That, therefore, he that runs races with goblin troopers, is likely to have rough riding of it:

"Ergo, for a country schoolmaster to be refused the hand of a Dutch heiress, is a certain step to high preferment in the state."

The cautious old gentleman knit his brows tenfold closer after this explanation, being sorely puzzled by the ratiocination of the syllogism; while methought the one in pepper and salt eyed him with something of a triumphant leer. At length he observed, that all this was very well, but still he thought the story a little on the extravagant—there were one or two points on which he had his doubts.

"Faith, sir," replied the storyteller, "as to that matter, I don't believe one half of it myself."

D.K.

—1820

In Context

Responses to *The Sketch Book* in American and British Newspapers

Irving's collection was warmly welcomed on both sides of the Atlantic, both as it appeared in several numbers beginning in 1819 and when it was published as a complete book. As was common throughout most of the nineteenth century, newspapers often reprinted reviews and commentary that had originally appeared elsewhere. And—again as was common at the time—American newspapers took particular notice of what was being written about American authors overseas. So too—as the last of the excerpts below illustrates—did English papers pay attention to what was written abroad.

from the *Recorder* (Greenfield, Massachusetts), 27 July 1819

Following the review (reprinted from the *New York Evening Post*), the *Recorder* printed Irving's "The Wife," accompanied by effusive praise: "... in our opinion, it is one of the finest eulogiums on the female character we have ever seen. It is beautifully pathetic, and will be read with interest, and, we hope, with benefit, by many."

LITERARY NOTICE.—A new work has been published by G. S. Van Winkle, entitled "*The Sketch Book of Geof frey Crayon, gent.* No. 1 "—This is a new production said to be from the elegant and racy pen of Washington Irving Esq. This first number contains five distinct sketches, viz: a sketch of Mr. Crayon; a sketch of a sea voyage; a sketch of Roscoe, the historian; a sketch of a wife; and a sketch of low life in an inland Low-Dutch village, as it appeared some sixty or eighty years ago, and which is thrown into the form of a story, entitled Rip Van Winkle. The graces of style; the rich, warm tone of benevolent feeling; the freely flowing vein of hearty and happy humor, and the fine eyed spirit of observation, sustained by an enlightened understanding, and regulated by a perception of fitness—a tact —wonderfully quick and sure, for which Mr. Irving has been heretofore so much distinguished, are all exhibited anew in the Sketch Book, with freshened beauty and added charms.

N. Y. Ev. Post.

from the *Knoxville Register* (Knoxville, Tennessee),
9 May 1820

Blackwood's Edinburgh Magazine,
for February last, contains a review of
the Sketch Book. The following ex-
tract from this review will serve to
show the estimation of this work a-
broad.

" Washington Irving, as yet a young
man, and who is at this moment in London, is a man of much more happy and
general order of mind than Brown, author of Wieland, Ormond, Edgar Hun-
tley, &c. & his works are much greater favourites among his countrymen
than the best of Brown's ever was.
He is the sole author of the Sketch
Book, a periodical work, now in the
course of publication at New York,
from which numerous extracts have appeared in the Literary Gazette, and
in many of the Magazines—none of
which however, seem to have known
from whose genius they were borrow
ing,so largely. We are greatly at a
loss to comprehend for what reason
Mr. Irving has judged fit to publish
his Sketch Book in America earlier
than in Britain; but, at all events, he
is doing himself great injustice, by not
having an edition here of every number after it has appeared at New-York.
Nothing has been written for a long
time, for which it would be more safe
to promise an eager acceptance. The
story of Rip Van Winkle; the Country Life in England; the account of
his voyage across the Atlantic, and
the Broken Heart, are all in their se
veral ways, very exquisite and classical pieces of writing, alike honorable to
the intellect and the heart of the author."

from the *Newbern Sentinel* (New Bern, North Carolina),
12 August 1820 (reprinted from the *Boston Intelligencer*)

It is delightful to read the effusions of a man of genius, whose mind is imbued with the colours of nature, and whose heart is susceptible of the most delicate impressions. —Full of ingenious and pertinent ideas upon a variety of interesting subjects, which he illustrates with beauty and elegance—and abounding with happily chosen expressions, Mr. WASHINGTON IRVING, the author of the Sketch Book, is the most fascinating of American writers.— Simple in his language, pure in his taste as well in the selection as the management of his subjects, and alive to the influences of internal and external nature—he affects the mind of the reader by the combined propriety and force of his remarks, and touches the heart by the pathos of his unaffected eloquence.

His wit and humour, without the smallest particle of grossness, are remarkable for exquisite acuteness of thinking, and a very extensive and minute observation of the ludicrous in mankind. He is equally fortunate in striking the mournful chord of the lyre ; or with his flying fingers to kiss the strings into merriment.

It would be difficult to discover an essayist in the whole catalogue of authors on polite literature of the present day, who unites more requisites for popular favour and whose popularity will more surely survive him. —Without the slightest air of pretension, his stories contain only a few simple but affecting incidents, and derive their deep interest, from the enthusiasm of feeling and the graces of diction with which he has enveloped them.

from the *Morning Chronicle* (London, England),
14 November 1821

The *Constitutionnel* was a Paris-based newspaper, founded in 1815 as
the *Independent*.

It would be rather unfair to hold Mr. WASHINGTON IRVINE responsible for the following puff which one of his friends has inserted in the *Constitutionnel*, and which cannot fail to excite a smile in most of our readers :—

The English, who cannot deny that their brethren beyond the Atlantic equal them at least in liberty and political intelligence—that they are able to struggle successfully with the mother country in what regards the progress of commerce, industry and agriculture, and that they surpass it efficaciously enough in the generous views of their diplomacy, entrenched their pride behind their literary superiority, and plumed themselves on the circumstance of the United States having, with the exception of FRANKLIN and BARLOW, produced as yet no man worthy of taking his place in the rank of the English classics of the reign of ELIZABETH and ANNE. This last resource has been taken from them. An American, Mr. WASHINGTON IRVING, *has raised himself by a single work* to the level of the purest and most elegant writers produced by England.

Irving's German Source for "Rip Van Winkle"

The following tale was recorded by German theologian Johann Karl Christoph Nachtigal in his 1800 collection *Volcks-Sagen*, or *Folk Tales*, but the original story is probably, like most folktales, much older. While he was living in England, Irving was introduced to a variety of English folkloric works by Scottish Romantic writer Sir Walter Scott. The influence of these on Irving's writing can be most obviously seen in comparing "Rip Van Winkle" to its counterpart in Nachtigal's collection, "Peter Klaus"; indeed, some passages of "Rip Van Winkle" appear to be close paraphrases of passages from Nachtigal's story. Some critics during Irving's lifetime accused the American author of plagiarism; Irving defended himself from such accusations, claiming that "popular traditions" such as folklore were "fair foundations for authors of fiction to build upon."

Peter Klaus[1]

Peter Klaus, a goatherd of Sittendorf, who tended herds on the Kyffhauser mountain, used to let them rest during the evening in a spot surrounded by an old wall, where he always counted them to see if they were all right. For some days he noticed that one of his finest goats, as they came to this spot, vanished, and never returned to the herd till late. He watched him more closely, and at length saw him slip through a rent in the wall. He followed him, and caught him in a cave, feeding sumptuously upon the grains of oats which fell one by one from the roof. He looked up, shook his head at the shower of oats, but, with all his care, could discover nothing further. At length he heard overhead the neighing and stamping of some mettlesome[2] horses, and concluded that the oats must have fallen from their mangers.

While the goatherd stood there, wondering about these horses in a totally uninhabited mountain, a lad came and made signs to him to follow him silently. Peter ascended some steps, and, crossing a walled

---

1 Translated from the German by Charles John Tibbitts.
2 *mettlesome* Lively.

from *Rip Van Winkle*

... As he was about to descend, he heard a voice from a distance, hallooing, "Rip Van Winkle! Rip Van Winkle!" ... He was surprised to see any human being in this lonely and unfrequented place, but supposing it to be someone of the neighbourhood in need of his assistance, he hastened down to yield it. ...

court, came to a glade surrounded by rocky cliffs, into which a sort of twilight made its way through the thick-leaved branches. Here he found twelve grave old knights playing at skittles,[1] at a well-levelled and fresh plot of grass. Peter was silently appointed to set up the ninepins for them.

At first his knees knocked together as he did this, while he marked, with half-stolen glances, the long beards and goodly paunches of the noble knights. By degrees, however, he grew more confident, and looked at everything about him with a steady gaze—nay, at last, he ventured so far as to take a draught from a pitcher which stood near him, the fragrance of which appeared to him delightful. He felt quite revived by the draught, and as often as he felt at all tired, received new strength from application to the inexhaustible pitcher. But at length sleep overcame him.

When he awoke, he found himself once more in the enclosed green space, where he was accustomed to leave his goats. He rubbed his eyes, but could discover neither dog nor goats, and stared with surprise at the height to which the grass had grown, and at the bushes and trees, which he never remembered to have noticed. Shaking his head, he proceeded along the roads and paths which he was accustomed to traverse daily with his herd, but could nowhere see any traces of his goats. Below him he saw Sittendorf; and at last he descended with quickened step, there to make inquiries after his herd.

The people whom he met at his entrance to the town were unknown to him, and dressed and spoke differently from those whom he had known there. Moreover, they all stared at him when he inquired about his goats, and began stroking their chins. At last, almost involuntarily, he did the same, and found to his great astonishment that his beard had grown to be a foot long. He began now to think himself and the world altogether bewitched, and yet he felt sure that the mountain from which he had descended was the Kyffhauser; and the houses here, with their fore-courts, were all familiar to him.

---

1   *skittles*   Form of lawn bowling, played with nine pins.

from *Rip Van Winkle*

On entering the amphitheatre, new objects of wonder presented themselves. On a level spot in the centre was a company of odd-looking personages playing at nine-pins. ... They all had beards, of various shapes and colours. ...

... [H]is knees smote together. His companion now emptied the contents of the keg into large flagons, and made signs to him to wait upon the company. He obeyed with fear and trembling; they quaffed the liquor in profound silence, and then returned to their game.

By degrees, Rip's awe and apprehension subsided. He even ventured, when no eye was fixed upon him, to taste the beverage, which he found had much of the flavour of excellent Hollands. He was naturally a thirsty soul, and was soon tempted to repeat the draught. One taste provoked another, and he reiterated his visits to the flagon so often, that at length his senses were overpowered, his eyes swam in his head, his head gradually declined, and he fell into a deep sleep.

On awakening, he found himself on the green knoll from whence he had first seen the old man of the glen. He rubbed his eyes—it was a bright sunny morning. The birds were hopping and twittering among the bushes, and the eagle was wheeling aloft, and breasting the pure mountain breeze. "Surely," thought Rip, "I have not slept here all night." ...

As he approached the village, he met a number of people, but none that he knew, which somewhat surprised him, for he had thought himself acquainted with everyone in the country round. Their dress, too, was of a different fashion from that to which he was accustomed. They all stared at him with equal marks of surprise, and whenever they cast eyes upon him, invariably stroked their chins. The constant recurrence of this gesture induced Rip, involuntarily, to do the same, when, to his astonishment, he found his beard had grown a foot long! ...

... His mind now began to misgive him, that both he and the world around him were bewitched. Surely this was his native village, which he had left but the day before. There stood the Kaatskill

Moreover, several lads whom he heard telling the name of the place to a traveller called it Sittendorf.

Shaking his head, he proceeded into the town straight to his own house. He found it sadly fallen to decay. Before it lay a strange herd-boy in tattered garments, and near him an old worn-out dog, which growled and showed his teeth at Peter when he called him. He entered by the opening, which had formerly been closed by a door, but found all within so desolate and empty that he staggered out again like a drunkard, and called his wife and children. No one heard; no voice answered him.

Women and children now began to surround the strange old man, with the long hoary beard, and to contend with one another in inquiring of him what he wanted. He thought it so ridiculous to make inquiries of strangers, before his own house, after his wife and children, and still more so, after himself, that he mentioned the first neighbour whose name occurred to him, Kirt Stiffen. All were silent, and looked at one another, till an old woman said—

"He has left here these twelve years. He lives at Sachsenberg; you'll hardly get there today."

"Velten Maier?"

"God help him!" said an old crone leaning on a crutch. "He has been confined these fifteen years in the house, which he'll never leave again."

He recognised, as he thought, his suddenly aged neighbour; but he had lost all desire of asking any more questions.

from *Rip Van Winkle*

mountains—there ran the silver Hudson at a distance—there was every hill and dale precisely as it had always been—Rip was sorely perplexed. "That flagon last night," thought he, "has addled my poor head sadly!"

It was with some difficulty he found the way to his own house, which he approached with silent awe, expecting every moment to hear the shrill voice of Dame Van Winkle. He found the house gone to decay—the roof fallen in, the windows shattered, and the doors off the hinges. A half-starved dog, that looked like Wolf, was skulking about it. Rip called him by name, but the cur snarled, showed his teeth, and passed on. This was an unkind cut indeed. "My very dog," sighed poor Rip, "has forgotten me!"

He entered the house, which, to tell the truth, Dame Van Winkle had always kept in neat order. It was empty, forlorn, and apparently abandoned. This desolateness overcame all his connubial fears—he called loudly for his wife and children—the lonely chambers rung for a moment with his voice, and then all again was silence. ...

The appearance of Rip, with his long, grizzled beard, his rusty fowling piece, his uncouth dress, and the army of women and children that had gathered at his heels, soon attracted the attention of the tavern politicians. They crowded around him, eyeing him from head to foot, with great curiosity. ...

Rip bethought himself a moment, and inquired, "where's Nicholas Vedder?"

There was a silence for a little while, when an old man replied, in a thin piping voice, "Nicholas Vedder? why he is dead and gone these eighteen years! There was a wooden tombstone in the churchyard that used to tell all about him, but that's rotted and gone too."

"Where's Brom Dutcher?"

"Oh he went off to the army in the beginning of the war; some say he was killed at the battle of Stoney Point—others say he was drowned in a squall, at the foot of Antony's Nose. I don't know—he never came back again."

"Where's Van Bummel, the schoolmaster?"

"He went off to the wars too, was a great militia general, and is now in Congress."

Peter Klaus

At last a brisk young woman, with a boy of a twelvemonth old in her arms, and with a little girl holding her hand, made her way through the gaping crowd, and they looked for all the world like his wife and children.

"What is your name?" said Peter, astonished.

"Maria."

"And your father?"

"God have mercy on him, Peter Klaus. It is twenty years since we sought him day and night on the Kyffhauser, when his goats came home without him. I was only seven years old when it happened."

The goatherd could no longer contain himself.

"I am Peter Klaus," he cried, "and no other!" And he took the babe from his daughter's arms.

All stood like statues for a minute, till one and then another began to cry—

"Here's Peter Klaus come back again! Welcome, neighbour, welcome, after twenty years; welcome, Peter Klaus!"

from *Rip Van Winkle*

Rip's heart died away, at hearing of these sad changes in his home and friends, and finding himself thus alone in the world. ...

... At this critical moment a fresh likely woman pressed through the throng to get a peep at the graybearded man. She had a chubby child in her arms, which, frightened at his looks, began to cry. "Hush, Rip," cried she, "hush, you little fool, the old man won't hurt you." The name of the child, the air of the mother, the tone of her voice, all awakened a train of recollections in his mind.

"What is your name, my good woman?" asked he.

"Judith Gardenier."

"And your father's name?"

"Ah, poor man, his name was Rip Van Winkle; it's twenty years since he went away from home with his gun, and never has been heard of since—his dog came home without him; but whether he shot himself, or was carried away by the Indians, nobody can tell. I was then but a little girl." ...

... The honest man could contain himself no longer. He caught his daughter and her child in his arms. "I am your father!" cried he—"Young Rip Van Winkle once—old Rip Van Winkle now! Does nobody know poor Rip Van Winkle?"

All stood amazed, until an old woman, tottering out from among the crowd, put her hand to her brow, and peering under it in his face for a moment, exclaimed, "Sure enough! it is Rip Van Winkle—it is himself. Welcome home again, old neighbour—why, where have you been these twenty long years?"

Images of Rip Van Winkle

John Quidor, *Rip Van Winkle and His Companions at the Inn Door of Nicholas Vedder*, 1839.

John Quidor, *The Return of Rip Van Winkle*, 1849.

The first illustrated edition of Irving's *Sketch Book* appeared in 1848, with seventeen illustrations by Felix O.C. Darley. (Irving contributed a new preface for the edition, but made no comment in it on the addition of illustrations to the texts.) Darley's one illustration for "Rip Van Winkle," which appeared without a caption, is reproduced here.

F.O.C. Darley, *Rip Van Winkle Awaking*, 1848.

Joseph Jefferson (1829–1905) became famous in the latter half of the nineteenth century very largely for his portrayals of Rip Van Winkle in the dramatic adaptation by Irish playwright Dion Boucicault (*Rip Van Winkle, or The Sleep of Twenty Years* [1865]); the play was a hit for many years in London as well as throughout America. The 30 September 1865 issue of *The Illustrated London News* featured the following short piece on the new play. The same issue included an illustration of Jefferson starring in the production. Both that image and a photograph of Benjamin Joseph Falk starring in the same role almost thirty years later are reproduced on the following pages.

The new play of "Rip Van Winkle," a dramatised version, by Mr. Dion Boucicault, of Washington Irving's most genial and humorous story—in which the hero, one of the early Dutch settlers in New York, falls in with the goblins who haunt the Katskill mountains, and drinks their magic liquor, causing him a sleep of twenty years—is likely to have a long run at the Adelphi Theatre. The new American actor, Mr. Jefferson, who appears as Rip Van Winkle, seems as though he had created the character himself, so perfectly does he enter into the author's conception of the loose-lived, lazy, lounging fellow, who lets his wife turn him out of doors and then becomes the victim of the mischievous imps, with the ghost of the old pirate, Hendrik Hudson, at their head. Our Illustration shows the scene in which poor Rip Van Winkle is compelled to quaff the fatal potion.

Scene from "Rip Van Winkle" at the Adelphi Theatre, 1865.

Benjamin Joseph Falk as Rip Van Winkle, c. 1894.

From the Publisher

A name never says it all, but the word "Broadview" expresses a good deal of the philosophy behind our company. We are open to a broad range of academic approaches and political viewpoints. We pay attention to the broad impact book publishing and book printing has in the wider world; for some years now we have used 100% recycled paper for most titles. Our publishing program is internationally oriented and broad-ranging. Our individual titles often appeal to a broad readership too; many are of interest as much to general readers as to academics and students.

Founded in 1985, Broadview remains a fully independent company owned by its shareholders—not an imprint or subsidiary of a larger multinational.

To order our books or obtain up-to-date information, please visit broadviewpress.com.

broadview press
www.broadviewpress.com

This book is made of paper from well-managed FSC® - certified forests, recycled materials, and other controlled sources.